CONQUEST:

THE STORY OF PIERRE RADISSON,

FOUNDER OF THE HUDSON BAY COMPAY

H. BEDFORD-JONES

CONQUEST

THE STORY OF PIERRE RADISSON,
FOUNDER OF THE HUDSON BAY COMPANY

H. BEDFORD-JONES

ALTUS PRESS • 2016

PUBLISHING HISTORY

Conquest: The Story of Pierre Radisson, Founder of the Hudson Bay Compay was originally published by The David C. Cook Publishing Company in 1914.

THANKS TO

Gerd Pircher

FOREWORD

The story of Pierre Radisson, which is herein related, has passed into history. That he was the first white man to reach the Mississippi, after De Soto, is now admitted. It was he who founded the Hudson's Bay Company, and who opened up the great Northwest to the world, receiving the basest of ingratitude in return.

The materials and facts used in this narrative I owe in part to Agnes C. Laut, who has rescued him from oblivion and given him his rightful place in history. The manner of his death no man knows to this day, but it is hard to imagine this world-wandered dying in his bed in London town; one likes to think of him as finding the peace of his "heart's desire" in the far land which he knew and loved and served so well.

—H. BEDFORD-JONES

DEDICATED

To my mother, whose picture is the picture of Ruth Mac-Donald in these pages.

CHAPTER I

WHAT WE FOUND ON THE MOOR

MY FATHER cocked up one eye at the heavens and stroked his heavy beard, and, as the storm was all but over, he growled assent in the Gaelic tongue that we of the west used among ourselves.

"Aye, come along, Davie. We'll have work to find the sheep and get them together after this blow. Belike they are huddled up in some corner of the moor—over beyond the Glowerie-gap, no doubt."

So blithely enough I whistled to Grim, and the three of us set off across the moors, while mother stood at the door and waved us a cheery farewell. Little she thought what burden we would fetch back with us that day! The great storm had blown itself out, and as we went along I asked permission to go down by the cliffs that afternoon and hunt for washed-up wonders of the ocean.

"Not you, lad," replied my father in his stern fashion, yet kindly enough. "There is work and to spare at home. Besides, the cliffs are no place for you this day. There'll be wreckers out betwixt here and Rathesby."

So with that I fell silent, wishing with all my heart that I might see the wreckers at work. For I was but a boy of nine and the life of a wrecker seemed to me to be the greatest in all the world. Little I knew of the sore work that was done along the west coast that day!

Years before, my great-grandfather, a MacDonald of the isles, had come across to the mainland and settled on Arby farm, and on this same stead I had spent my nine years. All my life had been one of peace and quietness, but I knew full well that the old claymore hanging beside the fireplace could not say as much.

For my father, Fergus MacDonald, had married late in life and my mother had come out of' the south to wed him. I had heard strange whispers of the manner of that wedding. It was said, and my father never denied it, that he had been one of those who, many years before, had hoisted the blue banner of the Covenant and ridden behind the great prophet Cameron, even to the end. Then, when the Covenant was shattered by the king's troops, he had fled into the hills of the south, and when the hunting was done and a new King come to the throne, he had brought home as his wife, the woman who had sheltered and hidden him in her father's barn.

How true these things were I never knew, but my father's fame had spread afar. In this year of grace 1701 the days of the Covenant were all but over. The order of things was shifting; rumors were flying abroad that the Stuart was coming to his own ere long, and that all wide Scotland would rise behind him to a man.

Of this my thoughts were busy as we strode over the heather, side by side. Grim following us sedately and inconspicuously, as a sheep dog should when he has age and experience. I always respected Grim more and liked him less than the younger brood of dogs, for he seemed to have somewhat of the dour, silent, purposeful sternness of my father in his nature, and was ever rebuking me for my very boyishness.

"Come, Davie," said my father suddenly, "we'll cut off a mile by going down beside the cliffs. Like enough we will strike on a few of the lambs among the bowlders, where there would be shelter."

This set my mind back on the sheep once more, and I followed him meekly but happily to the cliff-path over the sea.

Fifteen miles to the north lay the little port of Rathesby, and on rare occasions I would go thither with my father and enjoy myself hugely, watching the fishermen and sailors swaggering through the cobbled streets, and hearing strange tongues— English and Irish, and sometimes a snatch of Dutch or French. I knew English well enough, and south-land English at that, while my mother had taught me a good knowledge of French; but the honest Gaelic was our home speech and this I knew best of all, and loved best.

Our path, to give it that distinction, followed the winding edge of the cliff, where many a gully and ravine led down to the beach below. I cast longing glances at these, and once saw a shattered spar driving on the rocks, but was careful to betray naught of the eagerness that was in me. When my father Fergus had once said a thing, there was no naysaying it, which was a lesson I had learned long before.

Of a sudden Grim made a little dash around me and planted himself in the path before us. He made no sound, but he was gazing across the moors, and to avoid stepping on him we stopped perforce. It was an old trick of his, thus to give us warning, and I have heard that in the old days Grim and Grim's father had accompanied more than one fleeing Covenanter safely through the hills to shelter.

Now these tales leaped into my mind with full force at a muttered exclamation from my father, and I saw a strange sight. The sun, in the east, was just breaking through the storm clouds, lighting up the rolling heather a quarter-mile beyond us. There, full in its gleam, was a tiny splotch of scarlet.

The old days must have returned on my father, for as I glanced at him I saw his hand leap to his side. But the old claymore hung there no longer, and his face relaxed.

"What is it, Grim?" he said kindly. "Yon is a scarlet coat right enough, lad, but scarlet coats hunt men no longer over the moors. What make you of it, Davie?"

My father gave a cry of amazement.

"No more than you, father," I replied, proud that he had
appealed to me. The crimson dot was motionless, and no farther
from the cliffs than we. So, with a word to Grim, we walked
along more hastily, the sheep clear forgot in this new interest.
Scarlet coats were uncommon in these parts, and little liked.
As we drew nearer we began to see that this could be no man,
as at first we had thought, nor yet a woman. Indeed, it seemed

to be a garment flung down all in a heap, and I stared at it in vain.

Then the sun outburst all around us. As it did so, the crimson thing yonder seemed to be imbued with life, and my father gave a cry of amazement.

"A lassie! Now, where can she—"

Without finishing, he broke into a run, and I followed excitedly, for the figure was plainly that of a little girl. But what a girl! She was no more than mine own age, and the scarlet cloak fell from neck to heels about her as she came to meet us. Over the cloak was streaming a mass of yellow hair that seemed like spun gold in the sunlight, and presently I slowed my pace to stare at her.

Young though I was, I noted a peculiar quality in her as she ran to meet my father with outstretched hands, tears still upon her cheeks. I know not how to describe this quality, save that it was one of absolute faith and confidence, as if she had been waiting there for us. Old Grim hung behind, seemingly in doubt, but my father caught the lassie to him, which in itself was quite enough to make me all the more amazed.

"Why, the bairn's gey weet!" he cried out in the Scots dialect he seldom or never used. And with that I came up to them, and saw that in truth she was dripping wet. In reply to my father's words she spoke to him, but not in English or Scots, nor in any tongue that I had ever heard.

Bewildered and somewhat fearful, my father addressed her in honest Gaelic, but she only stared at him and me, her arms cuddled around his beard and neck in content. Then, to my further surprise, she laughed and broke out in French.

"You will take me home, gentlemen? Have you seen my mother?"

By the words, I knew her for a lady, and stammered out what she had said, to my father. He, poor man, was all for looking at her bonny face and stroking her hair, so I bespoke her in his place.

"Home? And where have you come from? Where is your mother?"

At this her lips twisted apprehensively, whereat my father cried out on me angrily; but she came around right bravely and made reply.

"We were going back to France, young sir. And my mother was in the boat."

"In the boat!" I repeated, the truth coming upon me. "Then how came you here?"

"Why," she returned prettily, "it was dark, and the big waves frightened poor mother, and I fell in the water and got all wet. Then I climbed out and looked for mother, but could not find her."

I put her words into Gaelic, staring the while at her cloak-clasp, which was like a seal of gold bearing a coat of arms. But when my father heard the story he drew her to him with a half-sob.

"Davie, the lassie came ashore in the storm! Take Grim and run down to the beach. If you find any others, men or women, bring them home. And mind," he flung over his shoulder savagely," mind you waste no time hunting for shells and the like!"

He swung the little maid to his shoulder, bidding Grim go with me, and so was striding off across the moor before the words were done. I stared after the two of them, and the lass waved a hand to me gayly enough; but as I turned away I felt something grip on my throat, for well I knew what her story boded. Many a good ship has been blown north of the Irish coast and full upon our cliffs, from the time of the great Armada even to this day, and few of them all have weathered the great rocks that strew our coast from Bute to Man.

There was little hope in my mind that I would find anything left of that "boat" the maid spoke of, but I called Grim and started for the nearest gully leading down to the shore. Soon the rocks were towering above me, and the beat of the surf thundered ahead, and then I entered a little sheltered cove where I had gathered shells many a time.

Almost at my feet there was a boat—a ship's longboat, rolling bottom side up on the rocks. I stood looking around, but could see no living thing on the spray-wet rocks that glittered black in the sunlight. Then Grim gave a little growl and pawed at something just below us. I felt a thrill, for more than once he had found in just such fashion the body of a dead sailor, but as I stooped down to the object rolling in the foam I saw it was nothing but a helpless crab washed up into a pocket. I pulled him out with a jerk and flung him back into the waves, turning away. The longboat was not worth saving, being battered to pieces, and if any of the crew had reached the shore they were not in sight.

So Grim and I returned home across the moor. How had a French ship come so far north, and on our western coasts too, I wondered? As we went, Grim found a score of sheep clustered in a hollow, so I hastened on and left him to drive the poor brutes home.

When I reached the house I made report of my errand, seeking some trace of the maid. But she was asleep in my own cot, and her crimson cloak was drying before the peat-fire, which seemed more like to fill it with smoke than dryness.

"Did you find who she was or whence?" I asked my mother, knowing that she spoke the French tongue far better than I.

"The poor child knew naught," she replied, as she mixed a bowl of broth and set it to keep warm. "The only name she knows is Marie—

"Which will be spoke no more in my house," broke out my father with a black frown. "I doubt not the lassie's people were rank Papists—

"Shame on you, Fergus!" cried my mother indignantly, facing him. "When a poor shipwrecked bairn comes and clings her arms about your neck, you name her Papist—shame on you! Begone about your business, and let sleeping dogs lie, Fergus

MacDonald. Cameron and Claverhouse are both forgot, and see to it—"

But my father had incontinently fled out the door to get in the sheep, and my mother laughed as she turned to me and bade me give the red cloak a twist to "clear the peat out of it."

Now, that was the manner of the coming of the little maid. Two days later my father took me to Rathesby with him to seek out her folk, if that might be. But no tidings had been brought of any wreck, and the best we might do was to write—with much difficulty, for my father was ever handier with staff than with pen—a letter to Edinburgh, making a rude copy of the arms on the gold buckle, and seeking to know what family bore those arms. No reply ever came to this letter, and whether it ever arrived we never knew.

And for this we were all content enough, I think. The lassie had twined herself about my mother's heart by her winning ways, and that confident, all-trusting matter laid hold strongly upon my father's heart, so that ere many weeks it was decided that she should stay with us until her folk should come to seek her.

I remember that there was some difficulty over naming her, for my father would have called her Ruth, which he plucked at random from the Bible on the hearth. I think my mother was set on calling her Mary, but the name of Mary Stuart was hard in my father's memory, and he would not.

So the weeks lengthened into months, and the months into years, and ever Ruth and I were as brother and sister in the farmstead at Ayrby. She learned English readily enough, but the Gaelic tongue was hard for her, which was great sorrow to my father all his days.

CHAPTER II

GIB O' CLARCLACH

SEVEN OF those years were the happiest of all my life,
perhaps. Ruth and I dwelt quiet at home, and between
whiles of the work my mother taught us much that we had
never known else. She was of good family, of the Eastoun Errols,
and how she came to love my father, who was rough and rude,
was always something of a mystery to me. But love him she
did, and he her, and it was a bad day for Fergus MacDonald
when my mother died.

This happening took place seven years after the coming of
Ruth, and was a sore grief to all of us. I never realized just how
sore a grief it was to my father, Fergus, until later. She was
buried beside those of the Covenant who had escaped the
harrying to die in peace, and I mind me that it was on a cold,
gray day which gave us little cheer.

The elder, old Alec Gordon, had carried pistol and sword at
Ayrsmoss, being given to preaching later in life. His mind was
a bitter one, setting well with that of my father, and this clay
of my mother's funeral gave me a distaste for the men of the
Covenant that I never outgrew. When it was all over I crept
away and went down to the cliff-edge, where Ruth presently
joined me, and we sat along with the heart-hunger that was
eating at us until the night-mists warned us home.

For many days thereafter my father spoke few words, and of
a sudden his age had come upon him, together with a strange
unrest that I had not seen in him before. But still we abode

there on the old farm until I was almost nineteen, and Ruth, as we guessed, a year younger. Then came the first of those strange happenings that led us so far afield and drew us into so weird a strand of Fortune's net before we had done.

Two years after my mother's death, my father began to have a succession of visitors. There was much talk in those days of the new lands over sea, and the rich farms to be had there for the taking. From what scattered words that came to us, Ruth and I judged rightly enough that these folk were talking of the plantations to my father, and so indeed it proved. Alec Gordon was the most constant visitor, and in time it came out that he would make a settlement in the new world, of a number of our folk. My father was much taken with the scheme, as were Muckle Jock Grier and Tam Graham, and others of the families nearby. At length my father announced that the next day but one Ruth and I should go with him to Rathesby.

His temper was dour and sullen in these days, and I dared not question him overmuch, but Ruth got the truth of the matter out of him on the way to town. It seemed that the elder, Alec Gordon, had prevailed upon a dozen families to carry the Covenant to the New World, and there to found a settlement to the glory of God, where there would be none to interfere or hinder, and where, as my father put it, "a new folk might be given growth by the Lord's grace, free from the temptations of the world and the wiles of the devil." But there were more devils in the New World than my father or old Alec wotted of.

I think he was much moved to this end by thought of Ruth and me, for he was earnest that we should follow in his footsteps and grow up God-fearing, respected young folk such as Lang Robin Grier. Now I ever was, and am still, I trust. Godfearing; but sour faces were little to my liking, and ranting Lang Robin much less. I mind me that when Robin would have impressed some doctrinal point upon Ruth, with many wise sayings and much doubting that her mind was sound in the faith, I went home with sore knuckles, and Robin went home with a sore face and a story that wrought much discredit upon me. Howbeit, to my tale.

We rode into Rathesby, where my father was to see Wat Herries, the master of the stout lugger that sailed to Ireland and France and beyond, and that even then lay in Rathesby bay. Smaller vessels than the "Lass o' Dee" had passed overseas in safety, and my father trusted in the hand of God more than he trusted in the hand of Wat Herries.

It was still early morn when we reached the port and put up our ponies at the Purple Heather, kept by old Gib Lennox. Then my father told me to wander at my will, taking good care of Ruth and returning at midday, while he strode off in search of Master Herries. The "Lass," we found, was newly come from France, and in her crew were many dark-faced fellows whose tongue sounded sweet in the ears of Ruth, so that we had to stop more than once and listen.

In the front of her cloak, now a modest gray one, she wore that same brooch with which she had come to us. I had hard work to keep her from speaking to the strange men in their own tongue, but after a time we came to the edge of the town and sat there among the rocks, well content to watch the lugger in the harbor and the fishing boats that lay around her.

As we sat there two men came strolling by—two of the sailors whom we had seen in the town. One was ordinary enough, the other a not ill-favored rogue save for deep pock-marks on his face that bespoke the plague, and a roving, cunning eye that bespoke a shifty soul. These passed so close that their talk floated to us, and naught would do Ruth but that I must call them over so that she might speak to them in French. Whereat, somewhat sullenly, I obeyed, and the men strolled across the shingle to us.

"And what might you wish, pretty maid?" asked the pock-marked fellow civilly enough.

"I but wished to hear the French tongue, sir," she replied with a smile. "It is long since I have spoken it—why, what is the matter?"

For a sudden the man had given a little start, his eyes fixed on her throat. Then he stared into her eyes, and at the look of him I half gained my feet.

"Your name?" he asked quickly. "What is your name, little one?"

"What is that to you, fellow?" I made hot answer, angry at his insolence. But Ruth caught my sleeve and pulled me down.

"Nay, Davie! Why should he not know? It were but civil to speak him fair, after calling to him. My name is Ruth, Ruth MacDonald," she added in French. At this it seemed to me that the man stared harder than ever, a puzzled look in his face.

"And how come you to speak our tongue?" he said, smiling quickly, so that I lost my anger. "It is strange to find one on these coasts who speaks so well and fluently!"

Ruth replied that she had had good teachers, and after a few words more the men walked on. But I noted that the one we had spoken with flung back more than one glance, and I was glad when midday came and we made our way back to the inn to eat.

There we found my father in deep converse with Master Herries, a hearty man of some two-score years, and straightway all thought of the two seamen fled my mind. For now the talk was all of lading and cargo, of whether sheep might be fetched in the lugger and of how many persons might sail with her. My father was set on taking with us as many sheep as might be, notwithstanding Wat Herries told him there was little sheep-land in the plantations.

While we ate and listened, Alec Gordon came in and brought a list of all those who had covenanted to go on the "Lass." The price was then agreed on, and much against my will my father bade me take Ruth forth again for an hour or two, as the inn was filling with seamen who drank much and talked loud, and there was but the one room.

So down to the sea we went once again, having had our fill of the town-sights, and wandered south along the low cliffs and the shore. Luckily enough, as it chanced, I picked up a water-clean cudgel that lay among the rocks and used it in sport as a staff. A bit after, I espied a small cuttlefish washed into a pool, and swooped down on the place in delight. But Ruth, who cared little for such creations as had snaky arms and hideous aspect, rambled onward among the rocks.

I was much concerned with my find, and had great sport. Once the foot-long arms were wound around that stick of mine, the creature would not let go, even though I beat him gently against the rock. I had no mind to lose the cudgel by leaving it there, and neither had I cruelty enough to crush out the life of the ugly creature, so I stayed and fought gently with him and forgot the passage of time.

On a sudden came a faint cry to my ears and I heard my name as if called from far away. Looking up, I saw no one and remembered that Ruth had gone on alone. Thinking that she had fallen into some pool among the rocks, mayhap, I caught up the stick, cuttlefish and all, and ran to the point of rocks that hid the farther shore from me. And there I gave a great cry of anger and amazement.

For, a quarter of a mile distant, I saw Ruth being carried up the cliff by two men. Though I could not see them well, for they were in the cliff-shadow, I remembered the two seamen instantly. Without pausing to think, I ran swiftly back to a little path that led up the cliff, in white anger. I knew these parts well, and when I gained the crest I would be betwixt the three and the town.

In this thought I was right, for in my haste I had beat them to the cliff-top and was running toward them when they appeared. Plainly they had not counted on me, because as I appeared they seemed no little alarmed. Then when I drew near, there came a flash of steel in the sunlight and my heart stood still, lest they injure Ruth.

But whatever their intention, it was unfulfilled. Before I could get to them Ruth began to struggle, and broke away just as the knives gleamed. One of the rogues wanted to run, but the other called to him to stay steady and regain the maid when they had flung the boy over the cliff. This did not serve to calm me overmuch, and I must have clean forgot to fear their knives.

As I ran up, the one of them sprang, but I whirled around the cudgel, which the cuttlefish yet clung to. The swing of it flung him off, and while I was still a few paces from the seaman I saw the creature strike him full in the face, as though thrown from a hand-sling—though it was the sheerest good fortune. With a great shriek the man turned and made off, clutching at his face, and I saw no more of him after.

But with the second man, him of the pock-marks, I was right soon busied. Amazed as he was at the somewhat ludicrous fate of his fellow, he came at me evilly. With a quick motion I shortened the cudgel and stabbed him in the breast with it, the point of his knife just shearing through my shirt, but harming me not at all. Then I gripped him by the neck and wrist.

Now we MacDonalds have ever been accounted strong men, and although scant nineteen, my father was wont to say that I promised not to disgrace the family in my strength. That was no light praise from his lips, but I never knew the worth of it till I gripped that seaman in my two hands. The anger that was upon me for the sake of Ruth was so great that there seemed to be a red haze in my eyes, and then I realized that the man had dropped his knife and was all but limp. Whereat I lifted him up and threw him to the heather, where he lay quiet.

Then I knew that Ruth was hanging to my arm, pleading with me not to harm the man. I stared down at her, breathing heavily, and wondered what to do with him.

"Were you hurt, lassie?" I asked in haste.

"No, Davie. They came upon me suddenly, and I had but time to cry to you before they clapped a kerchief to my mouth and lifted me. At the top of the cliff I broke from them. But—oh, I fear me you have hurt this man sore!"

"And well enough for him," I responded grimly. "He is like to be worse hurt when my father lays hands on him."

"David! Surely they are punished enough!" she cried out. Looking down at her, I saw that her golden hair was streaming free and in her face was that same all-trusting look wherewith she had met us nine years before. The memory of that day struck me like a shock, so that I stared speechless. Just then the sailor groaned, rolled over, and sat up. I put my foot on his knife, debating whether to hale him to Rathesby or not.

"Let him go, David," pleaded Ruth. "Truly, they did me no harm, and if father knew of it he would be very angry. Do not tell him, Davie, for it can do no good and will only make him dour for days."

Now this was true enough, and when the flame of my wrath had quieted somewhat I was not over-anxious to kindle the flame again in my father's heart. So I looked down at the man and bade him stand up, which he did with a groan, rubbing his neck.

"Who are you," I asked sternly. "What was your intent?"

He glanced from me to Ruth, an odd gleam in his crafty eyes which liked me little. He seemed to hesitate before answering, though I had spoken in his own tongue.

"I am called Gib o' Clarclach," he replied surlily, in right good Gaelic. As I stared in amazement, he darted a venomous look at me. "But elsewhere I am known as The Pike," he added," and I have friends you wot not of, stripling. So best say no more of this."

"That for you and your friends," and I snapped my fingers. "What wanted you with this maid? Answer, or you lie in Rathesby gaol this night."

But all the answer I got was a mocking laugh, as the fellow sprang away and was gone down the cliff-path. I plunged forward, but Ruth's hand clutched mine and her voice pulled me back. "Nay, Davie! Leave him go and let us return—for—for I am afraid!"

And the little sob she gave held me to her more than her grip, so that I laid her head against my shoulder and comforted her until she smiled once more. But she did not smile until I had promised to say no word of the affair to my father Fergus.

CHAPTER III

THE "LASS O' DEE" SAILS

WE TALKED little on the way back to the town, but none the less I was wondering greatly. So this seeming Frenchman could talk good Gaelic speech, as well as chatter French! That set me to marveling, for he looked like a Frenchman right enough. And what he called himself—The Pike! Surely that was no name for an honest man to bear, considering what kind of fish the pike was, even had the very giving of such a name not been a heathenish and outlandish thing. I had heard that the heathen in the colonies were named after beasts and birds, and so I came to the conclusion that he must have lived overseas. His Gaelic, however, was not that of the west coast, but held the burn of the Highlands.

I kept all this thinking to myself for the next few days. No harm had been done Ruth, so no harm had come of it; though why they dared to carry off a Scots maiden so near home was more than I could explain. In the end I gave up the attempt, having other thing to busy myself with.

When we had reached the inn once more we found my father ready to depart. With him was sour old Alec Gordon, who would bide with us at Ayrby over night. They rode on ahead, and from their talking Ruth and I gained some inkling of the great scheme.

The "Lass" had been engaged to take over the expedition upon her return from the next cruise, which would be in a month's time. This would give us who were going plenty of time

to sell our farms and stock and to make all ready for departure.
As to selling these, there would be little trouble about that, for
the hill folk and those from the south would be glad enough
to take them over and pay ready cash. We of the west have
always been accounted poor folk, but even in those days it was
a poor farm indeed that did not have a leathern sack hidden
away beneath the hearth, with something therein to clink. The
days of Claverhouse had taught the west folk a stern lesson.

Neither Ruth nor I was greatly in favor of seeking the New
World. We had many a conversation about Gib o' Clarclach,
which usually resolved itself into wondering why he had stared
so at the golden brooch; and in the end Ruth placed it away
and wore it no more until our departure. She loved our home,
with its rolling moors and cliffs and mountains, and could see
no reason for change; for that matter, neither could my father,
except that, as I said before, he was restless and thinking about
our future state.

As for me, I was wild to stay. Most lads would have wanted
to cross the world, but not I, for there was great talk of the
Stuart in the air. My father, who held all Stuarts for Papists,
was bitter strong for Orange and the Dutch, but the romance
of Prince Charles was eager in me. There were constant rumors
that the French fleet was coming, that men were arming in the
Highlands, and that the clans and the men of the Isles were
up, but nothing came of it all and our preparations went steadily forward.

It was no light task in those days to go into the New World
and found a settlement there. We were to take a dozen sheep,
and my father refused to part with Grim, of course. All the rest
was to be handed over to my father's kinsman, Ian MacDonald,
together with the stead itself. Our personal possessions were
all packed stoutly in three great chests of oak bound with iron,
and into one of these went Ruth's little red cloak, that my
mother had kept always.

Those were sad days for us, were the days of parting. There
was ever something of the woman in my boy nature, I think,

for it grieved me sore to part with the things I had known all my life, but especially to turn over to strangers the things about the house that my mother had loved and used. There was a big crock, I remember, which she had used for making the porridge every morning, and Ruth after her; this my father would not let us pack, saying that broken pots would make poor porridge in the colonies.

"Then it shall make porridge no more," I replied hotly, and caught up the heavy crock. Ruth gave a little cry as it shattered on the hearthstone, and I looked to feel my father's staff. But instead, he only gazed across the room and nodded to himself.

"Let be, Davie lad. We cannot always dash our crocks upon the stones and start anew. Now fetch in some peat ere the fire dies."

Very humbly, and a good bit ashamed, I obeyed. I had not thought there was so much restraint in my father, of late.

To tell the honest truth, Fergus Mac-Donald, as the neighbors said, was "fey" ever since the death of my mother. He would take his staff and Grim and so stride across the moors, return home in the evening, and speak no word for hours. These moods had been growing on him, but the bustle and stir of our preparations seemed to wake him out of himself in some degree, for which I was duly thankful.

The day of sailing had been set for the end of May, in the year 1710. Alec Gordon rode over with the word that the "Lass" had returned and her cargo—which as all knew, was contraband—had been safely "run" farther down the coast. The Griers were already in Rathesby, with two or three other families, and old Alec was gathering his flock together for the voyage.

So early the next morning we shut up the stead for Ian to take charge when he would, and departed for ever, as it seemed. We rode but slowly, Grim driving the sheep steadily before him and us, until we came to a roll of the moor we paused for a last look at the old place. As we turned away I caught a sparkle on my father's gray beard and the sight put a sudden sob in my throat; as for Ruth, she made no secret of her tears. And thus we left the little gray house behind us and rode with out faces toward the west and the sound of the sea beating on our ears.

We came down to Rathesby at last and found the little port in wild confusion. In all, there were eight families leaving—the Griers, two Grahams, three of the Gordons, Auld Lag Hamilton and his sons, and our own little party from Ayrby. All that afternoon we were busy getting the sheep stowed away on board—which Wat Herries considered sheer foolishness, as I did myself—and for that night we put up at the Purple Heather, the women sleeping in the guest-rooms while we men rolled up in our plaids and lay in the great room down below.

There was much talking that night ere the rushlights were blown out, and I learned that our destination was to be the colony taken from the Dutch long before and renamed New York, where land might be had for the taking. Indeed, I learned for the first time that Alec Gordon had not gone into this venture blindly, but had procured letters to the folk there from others of the faith in Holland, so that we were sure of a goodly welcome.

There was one matter that troubled me greatly that night, and kept sleep from me for a long time. This was that while we were loading sheep aboard that day I had seen a face among Master Herries' crew, and it was the face of Gib o' Clarclach, as he called himself. I wondered at his daring to return in the "Lass," knowing her loading and her errand, and for a moment I was tempted to have a word with Herries himself on the matter. How-beit, I decided against it and thereupon fell off to sleep, concluding that the man had sufficient punishment already and that to pursue him for a past fault would be no worthy end. But in days to come I repented me much of this, as you shall see.

In the morning we made a hasty breakfast together, and assembled in the big room for a last prayer. It was like to be morning-long, and after taking due part for an hour I slipped quietly through the door; not out of disrespect, but out of sheer

*As we came closer to the little boat we
saw that she helf only one man.*

weariness, for Alec Gordon was famed for his long-windedness.
Master Herries and his men were waiting aboard the "Lass,"
but as I watched the ship from the bench outside the inn, I was
aware of a man calling my name and pointing.

Turning, I saw that he was directing me to the hillsides, and
there in the gleam of the sunlight I saw a dozen men riding
breakneck toward the port.

"Best get auld Alec out," suggested the fisherman, and the look of him told me there was more afoot than I knew. So, taking my courage in hand, I slipped in through the side door again and so up behind the elder, in the shadow of the big settle. Waiting till he had finished a drawn-out phrase, I leaned toward his ear.

"Alec Gordon, there be men riding hard down the moors."

It seemed to me that his face changed quickly, but not his voice, for he continued quietly enough.

"Tam Graham, lead your flock to the boats. Do you follow him, Fergus, and all of you make what haste is possible." With that he fell into the border tongue as they all looked up in amazement. "Scramble oot, freends!" he cried hastily. "The kye are in the corn!"

Now well enough I knew that for the old alarm-cry of the men of Cameron, nor was I the only one. There was a single deep murmur, and the Grahams poured forth into the street. After them came the rest of us, I falling in at Ruth's side behind my father, and we hastened down to the boats. I failed utterly to see what danger there could be, and cast back an eye at the riders. They were still a quarter-mile away, but coming on furiously.

In less time than it takes to tell, we were into the small boats and rowing out to the ship. As I scrambled up the side I could hear the clatter of hoofs on the cobbles, but above us there was a creak of ropes and a flutter of canvas. Then there came shouts from shore, but we could not hear the words and paid no heed.

"Hasten!" shouted Master Herries, roaring like a bull at the men, and we saw a boat pulling out from shore. It reached us just as our anchor lifted, and over the rail scrambled a stout man waving a parchment with dangling seals.

"Halt, in the Royal name!" he squeaked, and my father stepped out to him.

"What's a' the steer aboot?" asked my father quietly. At this I looked for trouble, for it was in my mind that whenever Fergus MacDonald had come to using the

Scots dialect, there had been doings afterward.

"Ha' ye permission to gan awa' frae Scotland?" cried the stout man, puffing and blowing as he glared around. "Well ye ken ye hae nane, Fergus MacDonald, an' since I hae coom in siccan a de'il's hurry—

"Be off," broke in my father sternly, pointing to the shore. For answer the fellow waved out his parchment spluttering something about the "Royal commeesioner" that I did not fully catch. But my father caught it well enough, and his face went black as he strode forward and lifted the stout man in both hands, easily.

"Say to him it wad fit him better to look to his ain life than ours," he roared, and therewith heaved up the man and sent him overside into the bay. Wat Herries cried out sharply to duck behind the bulwarks lest shot be flying, but there was none of that. I saw the stout man picked up by his boat and return to shore, shaking his fist vainly at the laughter which met and followed him; then the wind bellied out our sails and the voyage was begun. A little later it came out that news had spread abroad of our purpose and that the commissioner had wished to stop us, but for what reason I never knew.

My father conjectured shrewdly enough that we would have been sent elsewhere than to New York. However, we soon forgot that, for the whole party was clustered on the poop watching the purple hills behind us. The little port faded ere long into a solid background, for the breeze was a stiff one, and that after-noon we looked our last on Scotland. This was the occasion for another address and prayer from Alec Gordon, and this time I joined in right willingly. I had never been so far from land before, and the tossing of the ship made me no wee bit uneasy.

Nor was this lessened during the following days. Five in all I suffered, together with all the moor-folk, as I never want to suffer more. Ruth was free from the sickness, as was my father, but Maisie Graham, poor soul, came near dying with it. After the fifth day, however, I crawled out on deck a new man, albeit weak in the legs, and never knew that the sun could feel so good.

The next day thereafter I was almost myself again, and paid back the jests of Ruth with interest. She had great sport of my sickness, although to tell the truth she tended me with unremitting care and kindness, when my father would have let me be to get over it as best I could.

To confess it straightway, I gained greater respect for Alec Gordon in those days, and in those to come, than I had ever felt before. The sight of the great ocean around us and the feel of the tossing deck that alone kept us from harm, put the fear of God into my heart in good surety, so that I entered into the morning and evening meetings with new earnestness. Nor was it only while the danger lasted that I felt thus. I had seen the ocean full often, but I had never so much as gone out with a fishing-boat, and those first few days were full of grim earnestness that proved their worth in the end.

It was on the twelfth day out that the first untoward event happened, for one of the seamen cried down to us that he had sighted a small boat that was all but sinking. Sure enough, we on deck could descry a point of white ahead, and all of us gathered in eagerness as we drew up to her. Thus far we had had good weather, and by now even Maisie Graham was free of the sickness.

As we came closer to the little boat, which was no larger than a sloop, we saw that she held only one man. Then a sense of strangeness seemed to settle over us when we knew that this one man was old, his long white hair and beard flying in the wind, but he stood erect and tall at his tiller. The strangest thing of all was that his cranky old craft was headed west, into the ocean itself, instead of back toward the land.

At our hail he came about readily enough, for his boat seemed much battered and was half full of sea-water. Handling her with no little skill, he laid us aboard and sprang over the rail. As he did so, I heard some of the seamen muttering in Gaelic—something about one of the sea-wizards; but to this I gave little heed as we all hastened to surround the old man and to talk with him.

CHAPTER IV

THE MAN FROM THE SEA

A FINE-LOOKING MAN he was, too, despite his age. I put him down as three-score and ten, and found later that I had not been far wrong. His face was hard-set and stern, like that of some eagle, his nose finely curved, and his deep-set eyes—ah, what eyes those were! Never since have I seen eyes like his. They seemed to be gazing far off, even as they looked into one's own; they seemed to see some great vision not given to other men's sight, as in truth I believe they did.

His hair was snow-white, but very thick, hanging about his shoulders, and on his bronzed neck was tattooed some strange animal which I had never before seen. So we stood about him, staring, while Wat Herries cast off the little sloop and left her to sink as she would.

The stranger searched us with those great black eagle-eyes, but shook his head at Alec Gordon's Gaelic, and muttered something that fetched a joyful cry from Ruth, for it was in the French tongue.

"You are a Frenchman?" she inquired quickly, pushing to my side. The stranger glanced at us, then his great figure quivered as a tree shakes beneath the ax. I could have sworn that a tinge of red leaped into his pale cheeks and that he was gazing at the golden brooch which once more held Ruth's cloak, but he replied slowly and calmly in a musical voice:

"I speak French, mademoiselle, though I may not claim to belong to that nation."

"Who are you?" asked Ruth, "and what are you doing in that little boat?"

"As to my name, that matters not," he replied with a bow that could only have been learned in courts. "I was sailing to the west, and if I might thank your company for saving me from a leaky and all but disabled craft, I would fain do so through you."

Ruth put his words into our own tongue, somewhat disconcerted at his courteous aloofness, whereat Alec Gordon rubbed his chin, and bade us salute him courteously.

"Tell the man that he must e'en go to the colonies with us," he said, knitting his gray eyebrows. "If he will not tell his name, we care little. Ask him of his religion."

And so Ruth did. But at the question the old man straightened up and a flash of fire leaped into his wondrous eyes.

"Who are you that dare to question me?" he replied sternly and proudly. "As to my religion, that is my own affair. May I ask your name, mistress?"

"We are of Scotland, of the Covenant," she returned simply, giving her name. He frowned as if in perplexity. "Fear not," smiled the little maid, mistaking his attitude. "You are with friends, old man, and if you be not a Papist your religion matters not."

He laughed shortly, staring down upon her. "Not I, maiden. As to fear, I am more hungered than fearful, though I have felt fear often in my time."

As Ruth gave his words to the others and my father led him to the cabin, I turned over this speech in my mind and set him down, boylike, as a coward. Therein I made a grave mistake, as I found out ere long.

It was but natural that the stranger should make great talk among us all, and when- he returned on deck, his tall figure wrapped in a spare plaid of Tam Graham's, we gazed at him ever more eagerly. But he gave us little heed,; going- forward into the bow and sitting there upon a coil of rope, gazing out into the west as if the ship sped not fast enough for him. After a little, Ruth and I, being the only ones aboard who could speak French, save the sailors, came to him. He did not repel us—nay, there was something about the man that drew us both, and Ruth more than me; he seemed like one who had seen many strange things, and the secret that shone forth from his deep eyes half frightened while it attracted me. As for Ruth, she felt sorry for him in his loneliness and wished to talk her French also, for she ever held that my accent was most vile. . He gave us a kindlier welcome than I had looked for, and when he smiled all his sternness vanished and I knew on the instant that here was a man who had suffered and loved greatly, and who knew how to win love from other men. There was about him something of that same quality which Ruth so greatly possessed, the quality of drawing out the faith of others, of quiet trust and confidence. I was not to know for many long weeks what it really meant to love and be loved by him, but, as I perched on the anchor chains and stared frankly at him, I thought that it must indeed be hard to tell this man a lie.

"If you would speak English," he smiled in the southland speech, "I can converse well in that."

"Nay," and Ruth's laugh rippled out, "French is mine own mother-tongue, and seldom do I get a chance to use it."

"Are you French, then? With your name?" he asked quickly. Now, though I knew full well that Ruth had come there with no such thought, she poured out the tale of her coming to us over the moors, as she had heard it often from my mother and me. This surprised me all the more because as a rule she made light of it and claimed Ayrby for home, and my people for her people.

The old stranger listened to all her story, but he remained silent and fell to staring over the bowsprit again as if he had not heard. But I who watched him saw him try to speak, as it were, then stop suddenly and gulp in his throat.

"It is a strange tale," he replied after a little, "and I thank you for the telling, maiden. Know you whither we are bound?"

"For the New York colony," I replied, somewhat downcast that he had not trusted us in turn with his own tale. He must have read the thought in my eyes, for he smiled sadly and I felt emboldened to question him. "What is that mark on your throat?" I continued, gazing at the tattooed animal. "Is that some strange beast?"

"Aye, strange enough," he turned human all at once and laughed in my face like a boy. "It is a beaver, an animal of the New World and of the old, yet stranger never lived. You will see many a beaver-skin—aye, and sell them, too, perchance!"

"Then you have been in the New World!" cried out Ruth, settling down snugly at his side. "Tell us all about it, sir!"

"The tale would outlast the voyage," he said, looking down at her face. A sudden mad thought came into my mind, and before I thought to stay it, sprang to my lips.

"In the New World," I asked eagerly, "did you ever know a man who was called The Pike?"

The answer to that question was wonderful enough. With one quick motion he leaned forward and gripped my shoulder in a hand of iron; and when his eyes bored into mine own I all but cried out, so like pure flame was the look therein.

"What know you of him?" he asked bitingly, and his tone minded me of my father's when he had flung the Commissioner's man over the rail. In that instant I feared this old stranger as never in my life had I feared anyone, no, not even my father; and so I gave him all I knew of Gib o' Clarclach, without let or hindrance. While I spoke, his grip loosened, but his shaggy brows came down until they met.

"Lad," he said when I had made an end, "keep this maid from that man as if he were the plague itself! Let him not touch her, should you ever meet again, and if he so much as looks at her put your knife into him as into a dog gone mad!"

"Why, the fellow is aboard now," I answered in wonder, and in no little fear. But to my surprise the old man only turned and gazed out into the sunset once more, checking Ruth when she would have spoken.

"My children," he said very softly, "while I am here you are safe from this man, remember that. Nay, I would not harm him. I am an old man, but I have been where no other white man has been; I have been a ruler among men whose skins are not as ours, and I go even now to end my days among these people. He, also, has been among them, and I know not what evil he is about here; but it seems to me that the hand of God has drawn me to you and to this ship, lest you come to harm. Now leave me, my children, and count me ever as a friend of the best."

Hand in hand, like two frighted bairns, we left him and went aft in awe. When we were alone in the cabin, all the other folk being above, Ruth looked strangely at me and caught my hand.

"Davie, is he not a wonderful man? Do you like him?"

"I fear him," I replied honestly. "But I think I could even love him, an' I had the chance. He is some great man, Ruth, that I know!"

"I like him, too, and I am not a bit feared of him," she said earnestly. "Say naught to anyone of what he said, Davie, for I think he would trust us more than others."

Whereto I agreed willingly enough, remembering that shoulder-grip which still burned me. But that did not save me from much speculating to myself. First, why had the old man been sailing westward in a small and battered sloop, scarce fit for coast fishing? Second, what did he know of Gib o'Clarclach? And last and greatest—who was he? These questions drove through my mind as I went back to the deck, but it was long ere any of them were answered. All that evening I looked about for the face of Gib the sailor, but saw it not.

Oddly enough, that same night a terrific gale from the south came on us. Odd, because until then the weather had been perfect, and also because of what followed. It was such a gale as I had never known before, keeping up day after day and driving us ever west and north, for the poor little "Lass" could only run with a single shred of sail to keep her right end forward.

That was a hard time for all of us. Morn and eve we held assembly in the larger of the cabins, where we men slept, and Alec Gordon led us in prayer. At each of these meetings the old stranger attended, although he took no part himself, which my father liked but ill. During those days we younger men helped the crew pull and haul, but the others were cooped up in the cabin—and a dreary place it was. Alec and the rest kept up an everlasting argument on Effectual Calling and Reason Annexed, together with other such topics as the articles of faith afforded, and I was glad enough to be sharing with the crew instead of listening to such talk below, for I was ever fonder of action than discussion.

I had nearly forgot the other part of our crew and cargo— Grim, who kept company with half a dozen more sheep dogs, and the poor beasts stowed away in hasty-built pens below. The day the old stranger came aboard, three of the sheep died, and what with broken legs from the rolling of the "Lass," and from sickness, the rest followed speedily. Wherein Wat Herries was proved to know his business better than my father. As for Grim, he kept close below after the storm began, and remained there in safety, keeping near to my father's heels as usual.

For a week that storm blew down on us, and there was rest or comfort for none aboard. On the seventh day we had clear weather once more and returned to our course, from which we had been sadly driven. Two days after this befell a sore accident, for Master Herries was knocked down by a lower yard breaking from its cordage, and when we picked him up his right leg was found broken below the knee.

We carried him to his cabin and there my father, who had no little leechcraft, tended him. This placed the ship in the hands of an Ireland man called Black Michael, who was good enough in his way, but a poor mate, for as events proved he had little hold on the men forward.

As if this were not enough, the storm came back upon us the next day and again the poor "Lass" fled helpless before it. It was now that first I noted a peculiar manner among the men, who like all our west coast seamen were highly superstitious. I thought little of it, nor dreamt how it tended, until one night when I crept forward to steal a pannikin of water from the butt for Grim. On my way back I heard two seamen talking in Gaelic, behind a corner of the cabins, and the wind carried me their words.

"*Duar na Criosd!*" muttered one, an Irisher like the mate. "There is no doubt of it, Eoghan! I have seen it before, and I tell you that unless Ruadh has green stuff in plenty, he will die! It is the scurvy, and we have naught aboard to fight it with."

"Scurvy an' you like," replied the other sullenly, "but I say it is the old wizard whom we took aboard. Do you mind the tale of Jonah in the Scriptures? Do you mind how the sheep began to die when he came, and how he brought the gale with him?"

There was a little silence, and I felt my heart sound against my ribs as I began to comprehend their words.

"Like enough," answered the first with an oath. "But the scurvy is upon us, and we be all dead men, Eoghan, unless we fetch land right soon. Nor is the manner of that rotting death pleasant," and with this he described the workings of scurvy until my flesh creeped.

"Then let us have this Jonah overboard," cried out the other man on a sudden, and despair was in his voice. "Gib o' Clarclach is with us, and the rest. Black Michael matters not; put this wizard overside and we will have fair weather again. Who ever heard tell of such gales at this season?"

Which same was true enough, and I even wondered a trifle if the man might not be right.

"Stay," returned the first. "I have a better plan. The old wizard sleeps in the cabin aft, with the captain. I will slip in there this very night, when the watch is changed, and have my knife in him and out again. Let the elder lay it to the Lord's vengeance an' he will, being overfond of such talk."

At this the other man laughed shortly, but I crept very silently across the heaving deck to the cabin, and there was great fear in my heart for all of us.

CHAPTER V

HOW THE "LASS" WAS DRIFTED

O N H A N D S and knees, the deck beneath me groaning and pitching to the tossing of the great waves, and the howling wind still seeming to thrill those muttered words to me, I crawled on and with some difficulty, brought the water to Grim, who thanked me in his own way. Then I rose and looked about.

Around the table were lashed my father, Alec Gordon, and Robin Grier, all arguing at the top of their tongues. In the bunks lay the others, or on heaps of padded canvas along the floor. Then I understood that the old stranger had gone to Master Herries' cabin, where the mate sometimes lay also, and was caring for the injured man. Besides Grim there were five other dogs lying around, but the womenfolk were all safe asleep in their own place.

I misliked saying anything to my father and old Alec, for fear they would disbelieve me. Had Ruth been there I would have sought counsel from her, and have gained it, too; but a notion came to me that the work might be done without a quarrel. Had I told my father the tale, he might have sought out the two men and cracked their heads together, likely getting a knife in him for it. So, without disturbing any of the three at the table, I caught hold on Grim and drew him out of the cabin.

The master's, cabin, where were the old man and Wat, was but a miserable hole to one side of our main room, and had indeed been intended for some other use. It would be easy enough for a man to slip in and out again, I considered as I crossed the few feet of open deck to get to it, Grim holding back stiff-legged, in wild fear with each toss of the lugger. Then I cast open the door of the little place and went in, flinging Grim before me.

A roll of the ship assisted me in this, so that Grim and I went in together and fetched up against the old stranger, clean taking him off his legs. A ship's lanthorn swung above, and by its light the old man made out who we were, as we all rolled in the corner in a heap. For that matter, he had long since proved a better sailor than any of us on board, and now he was .on his feet instantly, and soon had me up.

There was little room for others when the door was shut, and I saw that the old man had been lying in the mate's bunk when we came. Above this lay Master , Herries, asleep in his own bunk despite all the uproar. Now, it had been in my mind to set Grim awatch, but when the old man smiled on me and asked my errand, I had blurted out the whole before I thought. At the story he threw back his head and laughed heartily, seeming to take it as a huge joke.

"Nay, lad, be not put out," he cried kindly, seeing that his laughter made me angry, and therewith clapped me on the shoulder. "I laughed not at you, but at them. Why, it is a rare jest indeed, their taking me for a wizard and thinking me over-side—belike it is the work of our friend, Gib, too. Bide you here, David, and methinks we will carry out that jest somewhat."

Pushing me and Grim into the corner, he reached up and blew out the lanthorn, then caught my hand in his and reached for Grim's head as we all settled down together. I had begun to feel fear of him, but when Grim suffered his petting I took heart and cast it off. Grim was a good judge of men, and allowed few to handle him as did this old stranger.

"This is not unlike a night I once spent in the Canadas," broke out the rich, musical voice of the old man. "It was deep winter, and I lay in a little cave with two of my red brothers, after escaping from a great town of the Ottawa nation. For you must know, lad, there are many races of these red men, each at war with the other."

"I know little about it, sir," I answered.

Methought he gave a little impatient sigh at that. "Lord, will these thick-headed English never learn where lies their greatest rulership? But no matter. My own people, among whom I was a chief, were named Mohawks, and we had been captured by the Ottawas after a great raid out to the westward. All of us were sore wounded and far from home, having no meat save two rabbits we caught, all during the two weeks we lay there.

"Well, on this night of which I speak we were all but frozen, and at length made shift to build a small fire. All around us were our enemies, and we had seen a dozen braves searching that same day. It was something like midnight when I, who was on watch, saw a tall deer pass—"

And more of that story I never heard, because just at that instant the door of the cabin opened very softly, and I almost thought it had been done by a lurch of the ship but for feeling Grim bristle. Then my hair stood on end with pure horror, for in the cabin above the timber-groan and howl of the wind, there came three shrill, clear hoots of an owl.

A dark shape which had filled the doorway suddenly paused. Grim began a growl, but I checked him at hearing a chuckle from the old man, and berated myself for a fool. It was his work, of course. But there in the dark it sounded eerie enough, and when two raven-calls echoed out I scarce repressed a cry. A ragged streak of lightning outside showed us the figure of a man in the doorway, others behind him, and the gleam of bare steel; then as the light passed I sprang up, for in my ears had shrilled up the long sobbing howl of a wolf—a sound to wake the dead!

Wake me it did, and Grim too, for he answered it with another and leaped away from me. We heard a startled yell from the men, and then the old stranger slammed the door before Grim could escape.

"Easy, old boy, easy! Wait a bit till we get a light."

With a dexterous flint and steel he soon had the lanthorn going, to my no small satisfaction. Wat Herries was still sleeping, which I wondered at. I was still blinking when the old man pulled me up and took my hands in his.

"Davie, lad," he said softly, "you did a good deed this night. Now begone, and fear not for me. Those devils yonder will come near me no more save in the light of day."

"But—but—I stammered fearfully," was it witchcraft or—

"Witchcraft? Forest craft, more like," he laughed, his white beard shaking at me. "'Tis a gift the Lord and the Mohawks gave me, but we will e'en give the Lord credit, Davie. So get you gone to sleep and breathe no word of this."

Much reassured at finding he had no dealings with the black art, though I deemed his speech not far from blasphemy, I caught hold on Grim and we both returned to the main cabin, where all was as we had left it and Alec Gordon still arguing stoutly. I flung down on a pile of canvas and went to sleep with Grim still in my arms, but that wolf-howl echoed through and through my dreams that night and I woke with it still in my ears. Indeed, it then seemed scarce a thing of this world, though I have since heard it often enough.

When I went on deck next morning we were in worse plight than ever, for it was biting cold and there were masses of ice around us, floating in the sea. I learned that we had been driven far north, where the seas are full of ice even in June, but it seemed a mighty strange thing to me. There was some fog also, and every now and then the "Lass" would heave her bows into an ice-cake with a shivering crash that boded ill for her timbers.

That day two of the womenfolk, both Gordons, complained of a new sickness, and Robin Grier said his teeth were loose in his head. My father and old Alec were puzzled enough, but when the stranger heard of it he ordered that the sick ones be given naught save green stuff to eat. That minded me of the talk I had overheard, but a warning glance from the old man checked the words on my lips. It was then we learned that many of the crew were sick likewise, of that plague called scurvy, which comes from eating no fresh green things. We were in sorry plight, for save a few potatoes our green stuff had all vanished long since.

That day there was no wind to speak of, and I drew Ruth up into the bows again, where we sat gloomily enough with plaids wrapped around to keep out the damp fog. I had seen Gib o' Clarclach once or twice, but he kept well out of my way and out of sight as much as might be. I told Ruth all that had taken place the night before, but at my fears of witchcraft and wizardry she laughed outright.

"Yet the old man said himself that he had been a chief among the red heathen of the Colonies," I argued, "while his speech was all but blasphemous."

Whereat she only laughed the more, and I grew sulky until she pointed to a little bunch of the crew in the shelter of the rail below us, in the waist.

"I am more feared of them than of any wizard, Davie," she said. "This terrible sickness is come upon us all, and we cannot fight against it. And see where we are come—up into the sea of floating ice! With Master Herries laid up in his bunk, and the men agog with superstition, we are like to have an ill time ere we reach the plantations."

"Just the same," I repeated stubbornly, "I cannot see how any one can be a chief among the heathen cannibals and still remain a God-fearing man. And why will he not tell his name, and whence he comes?"

This silenced Ruth for the time, and though she laughed again I could see that she was perplexed also. But with the contrariness of women she declared that the talk wearied her, and so changed the topic abruptly.

We lay idle for three days, with nothing save ice and fog around us. Then came another gale, this time from the east, and we began the weary fight once more. Strangely enough, my father and rugged old Lag Hamilton, with Alec Gordon himself, were now feeling the scurvy; and we were all of us frightened by it, and by our own helplessness. One of the dogs had been lost overboard, having ventured out on the deck in the storm, so thereafter I kept Grim safe inside the cabin.

Of the old stranger we saw little during those days. He was busy tending Wat Herries, which he did with the skill and tenderness of a woman, and we were all taken up with our own sick. Whenever I went on deck I saw that the crew obeyed Black Michael with a sullen, surly manner that boded ill. Many of them were sick also, and among these went Ruth with such small comforts as we had, till not a soul on board but loved her—save possibly one.

On the third day of that gale matters came to a head. I do not think any of us, save Ruth and I and the stranger, suspected that the crew had aught in mind; but had not my father been down with the plague I would then have told him all. The suspense was hard on me, almost too hard to bear. Day and night we had to keep watch, twice narrowly missing great mountains of ice, and on the third day we struck a water-lashed cake with such force that the "Lass" sprung a great leak.

When this was discovered the crew well-nigh went mad with fear. I was in the cabin when the crash came, and ran to the door with the others. When Black Michael ordered the men to the pumps, they rebelled flatly, and before he could so much as move he was trussed up like a fowl in one of his own tarred ropes. Then knives flashed out in the light and the men came surging aft. I cried out to Robin Grier and with our fathers' claymores, which we fetched from the cabin on the run, we stationed ourselves over the ladder at the break of the poop, and called on the men to halt. Tam Graham and those of the others who were not down with the sickness came out behind us.

With a sudden loathing I recognized the leader of the crew for Gib o' Clarclach. He stood looking up with his evil grin, but kept well out of reach of my weapon.

"Let us by, MacDonald," he spoke out. "We are acting for the good of all, and bring no harm to you and yours."

"That is a lie," I cried hotly. "I know well what you want, and you shall not pass by this ladder, you rebels! As for you, I have met you before now, Gib o' Clarclach, and know more of you than I did then. You got little good out of your visit the other night, and you will get little good now. Best stow away your knives and go about your work."

The only answer I got was a howl of rage from the men.

"The old wizard is Jonah!" yelled out the fellow called Eoghan, with a flourish of his long knife. "Put him into the sea again and let him go his way. He has bewitched us all, and we be dead men unless we rid the ship of him!"

This talk staggered Robin, who wavered and glanced at me, irresolute. Tam Graham muttered something behind me, and the men below yelled again and came at the ladder, seeing their advantage. But I would not give back, nor did I want to hurt any of them, so I brought down the flat of my father's claymore on Gib's crown, and tumbled him to the deck, whereat all drew back with a snarl.

As for Gib, he leaped to his feet and drew back his hand quickly. There came a flash of something, and Robin dashed me aside just in time to let a long knife fly under my arm. The scoundrel yelled something at me in a strange tongue, but before I regained my balance a sudden silence fell upon them all, and they stared past us. Turning, I heard a whispered prayer from Robin, and saw the old man.

He was standing just behind, a brass-bound pistol in each hand, his knees giving to the sway of the deck as the "Lass" pitched. Then a howl went up from the crowd below.

"Wizard!" they yelled, some in English and some in the Gaelic. "Get you gone and take your spells from us!" And they surged forward. But the old man raised his pistols, his white hair flying, and a fierce flame raging in his eyes. I think those eagle-eyes halted them more than the pistols, for they were in a mood to care little for two bullets.

"Fools!" he cried in English, and yet again. "Fools! Would you destroy your only hope? You dogs, I am Pierre Radisson!"

CHAPTER VI

RADISSON THE GREAT

"**R**ADISSON! PIERRE Radisson!"

At the muttered word and the blank look on the faces below I could have laughed, but I make no doubt that my own face looked as blank as theirs. Not a soul on board but knew that name, and in a flash it all came over me, till I flushed with shame at my own suspicions.

Out of the world as we had been at Ayrby, even I had heard this man's story. It was said that he was a French-Canadian by birth, and was the greatest adventurer of our own times. He had found a great river to the west of the Colonies, the same which Marquette and La Salle explored, and later on had opened up the Canadas to trade. He it was who had founded the Company of Gentlemen Adventurers into Hudson's Bay, the fame of which was great, and by the exploits of his arms had kept them there against the French.

But Radisson had found that the faith of princes is a weak rod to lean upon. First, the French had betrayed and robbed him, which had sent him over to England. Then, after the founding of the Great Company, the very men to whom he had brought fortunes had left him to starve, denying him all share in the huge profits they made in furs from the Canadas. My father had often dwelt on this story as an example of the faith of kings. Time and again Radisson had swept the Bay of French or English, but the ending of it all was that he was thrown upon the streets of London town. How Pierre Radisson came to be on board the "Lass," how he had come into that little, leaky sloop, I knew not; but as I gazed on the stern face of him I felt a sudden great thrill of hope and eagerness.

The rebels felt more than that, for they were mightily afraid of this man, who had single-handed done such deeds in the Canadas that all men had heard of him. I caught a quick oath from below, saw Gib o' Clarclach break away and vanish forward, and so finished the mutiny. With a little laugh Radisson put away his pistols.

"I will take charge of this ship," his voice thrilled along the deck. "Have no more of this foolery. Unloose the mate yonder and go to your places. By the help of God we will come safe to shore yet."

Very silently and in great awe the men unbound Black Michael, and in no long time the ship was as it had been. Robin and Tam Graham and I stood wondering at the break of the poop. Radisson turned to us with a courtly bow.

"Gentlemen, I thank you for your support. The crew is like to be short-handed ere we reach any port, and if need be I will call upon you for help," said he.

Robin stared, his mouth agape, and old Tam withdrew to tell the news in the cabins, whither we followed him presently. I looked about for Ruth, and found her giving some broth to my father and Alec. When this was done I took her out on deck willy-nilly, for she needed a breath of air and we cared little for the storm that still raged.

Since men were in the bows watching for ice ahead, we sat us down in the shelter of the cabin, and presently Radisson came thither and joined us.

"So now the mask is off," he said, speaking in French, and smiling. "I had not thought to tell my name, but it must needs out. We are in a bad strait, my friends."

"Why?" questioned Ruth. "And why not tell your name in the beginning? Surely you had no hard thoughts of us?"

Radisson looked sadly into her eyes, and smiled again. "My child, I have fled from England to die in mine own country. They would not let me go, they would not let me work for them nor serve them, and France has cast me out. Yet the English feared that I would serve France again, and so when I had provided for my wife and children I fled in secret to the coast and embarked in that little sloop wherein you found me.

"I had no hard thoughts, lass, but I am suspicious of all men. The wilderness is my only home, and it is to the wilderness that I go. If I come to the Colonies, or to New France, I shall be laid by the heels. They seem to fear that my very presence would work them ill." He lifted his face and looked to forget us as he gazed abroad into the storm. "Is there some curse upon me, Lord God, that men fear me so? Ah, to be once more on the open prairies where the air is free of plots, with red-skinned friends behind me and the unknown world ahead!"

Those words sank deeply into my mind, and there was to come a time when I would remember them again; but Ruth leaned forward and took his hand gently. A right strong hand it was, for all its age unwrinkled and firm as mine own.

"Nay, speak not so bitterly," she reproved him softly. "There is no curse upon any man, dear sir! Come, you shall go with us and join our settlement, and when all is safely bestead you shall go and come as you please, with none, to hinder!"

"So?" Radisson gazed down at her unsmiling, and I felt on a sudden that there might indeed be fear in his soul, but in no wise a selfish fear. "And whither is this ship sailing?"

"What—" Ruth stared up at him, her wonder slowly changing to something more. "You think—we are in danger?"

"Grave danger," he nodded confirmingly. "None know it save Wat Herries your master, and I, but we have been driven far from our course to the Colonies. Until I can get sight of the sun I know not whither we have drifted, but we are likelier to be near Greenland than the Americas."

This told us nothing, for we knew not that there was such a place as Greenland. There was no more trouble with the crew, who were all eager enough to do Master Radisson's bidding. But the scurvy was now upon us sore, all having it save Ruth and me and one or two others and Radisson himself. Two days later the storm ceased as suddenly as it had begun, and that noon Radisson and Black Michael busied themselves with poor Wat's instruments, until after an hour Radisson came below and asked to see Alec Gordon.

"Sir," he said quietly, while I held up old Alec's stricken head, "you must know that we are far off our course, and in dire need of green food, even if it be but grass. Now I know these waters well, and if we turn to our right course we will all be dead ere we reach the Colonies. But, an' it please you. I can guide this ship into Hudson's Bay and so to one of the posts established by the Adventurers. There we can remain till Master Herries be recovered and the sickness gone, when it will be no great matter for him to lay a course for the Colonies from there."

For a moment there was silence. We were all taken aback by this news and knew not what to say, until finally Alec sank back his head with a groan, speaking in the Gaelic which I translated.

"Do your best, Master Radisson, and we ask no more. The Lord hath sent you to us, and He knows His business best. "

So it came about that our prow was no longer turned to the south, but to the west. Now, too, the winds favored us and drove us onward full steadily, and the same day our course was determined on, one of the men found a sack of half-rotted potatoes in the hold. We hunted over, but found no more. These, however, served to stay the sickness in a slight degree, and seemed to the men to be a good omen.

For many days thereafter we stood forward with the ice all around and with the weather bitter, but without storms to hinder and harass us. In that time Pierre Radisson drew ever closer to me and to Ruth, sitting often with us and talking much of his travels and adventures, one hand on Grim and the other clasping mine or Ruth's. On one of these occasions I asked him about Gib o' Clarclach, called The Pike.

"The man is of your own country," answered Radisson, "though most of his life has been spent among the French. It was in New France I found him first, and he was a member of the party that went with me from Montreal to the fur country. He was but a lad then, and of evil ways, but a good fighter and of great resource. When we returned, our canoes deep-laden with a rich cargo, it was he who urged the Governor to seize the furs and betray me.

"After, I came to England. When next I came to the Great Bay whither we are now bound, this fellow stirred up trouble mere than once, for he was dwelling among the Chippewa nation, and he had become a powerful man among them. However, I was no less powerful among the Crees, and the Sioux to the far south, and on one occasion we trapped The Pike with many of his men. It was thought then that he was killed, but evidently he escaped to do more evil in the world. Long ago I swore vengeance against him, and that vow will some day be kept."

"But why did you not shoot him the day he led the mutinous men?" I queried. "If the man had done me so much harm—"

"Peace, lad," commanded the old man firmly, but kindly. "I am older than you, and such things I have learned to leave to a higher hand than mine own. Never fear, this man will meet his punishment as God wills, in God's own good time. Mind you not what the Scriptures say—"

"Aye, well enough," I broke in heatedly, thinking on my first meeting with the man. "But if the time ever comes when I stand against him again, I will strike with no flat blade then! And besides," I added shrewdly, "methinks there is more to the tale than you have told."

Radisson smiled. "Aye, lad, much more, but the time is not come for the telling, spitfire!"

"But, sir," cried out Ruth suddenly, "how is it that you are taking our ship into the Great Bay, when you feared so much to fall into the hands of these men? Will they not do you injury?"

"That may well be," answered Radisson quietly. "But I think God has sent me to do my utmost for you and yours, maiden. My own fate matters little, and it is even in His hands. I do not think He will let me come to grief while I serve Him, child."

Ruth said nothing to this, but she gazed at Radisson's sorrow-graven face with a great admiration, in which I shared to the full. And in truth it was no little thing to which he had set himself. Were it known that he was alive and in the fur country, the English and French raiders would both be after him. Both nations had wronged him deeply, and both feared and hated him equally; for as my father used to say, "If ye never do a man an injury, Davie, you'll aye live in brotherly love." Thus it was with the great Pierre Radisson.

He of all men had seen that there was an unsuspected greatness in the country north of the Canadas. He had discovered and opened up that country to the fur-trade, and had received little thanks for his pains. Even his wanderings in the far west were but little known, as he told them to us during the voyage. His brief tale of Gib had shown me much of the man's own greatness, for Radisson had spoken without bitterness or rancor, deeply as he had been wronged by the traitor and spy.

So, if he took the "Lass" into Hudson's Bay as he intended, and brought us safely to one of the Adventurers' posts, he would have little chance or none of getting away free himself.

Of all on board, I think that only Ruth and I understood this—save, mayhap, Gib o' Clarclach, of whom now we saw nothing at all. In the days that followed our talk with Radisson, I had no chance for another spare hour with Ruth. The illness had seized upon the crew until we were very shorthanded, and with those of our party who were able, I took place with the sailors at the ropes. There were but half a dozen of us all left untouched, and a few days later poor Maisie Graham died.

Her funeral was a gloomy enough matter, for my father, looking like some great gaunt specter, took the place of old Alec and afterwards staggered back to his bed again. Ruth and those others of the women who could, tended the sick. At morn and eve we gathered beside Alec and it was a fearsome thing to hear the words of prayer come from those blackened, disease-scarred lips. Yet those days of terror made a man out of me who had been a boy, and but for them I had never had the faith and courage to meet what came after.

So we drove east and south through the ice, great mountains of it all about us, trusting everything to the old man who led us on. Then one day there came a blue haze on the horizon, and a feeble yell of joy went up from the men. I looked to see Radisson turn us in toward the land, but he shook his head to my questions.

"Nay, lad, that is but a barren icebound coast. We must on into the bay itself and there, please God, we shall find peace."

But the news that we were come to the New World at last was wondrous heartening to our sick, notwithstanding that two of the men died that same day. The leak had gained greatly upon us, and the next morning I felt signs of the illness for the first time. Ruth had not been touched by it, and of the men only Gib, Radisson, and one or two others had escaped. But all the women, poor folk, were in their beds.

Then we came to the great cliffs, stern and icy. A day later a gale came down from the north and drove us onward into the bay; and although this increased the labor at the pumps, yet we welcomed it, since it but sent us the faster toward safety. And at length, as I came on deck at sunrise to take up my watch, I heard a hoarse shout from the weary men, and looking across the floating ice at the dark shore, saw a break of green that we had come to in the night.

CHAPTER VII

GRIM HOWLS

IT WAS an inhospitable shore, seen through the shreds of mist that were driving in on us, but never was a heartier prayer of thanks sent up than that which rose from the "Lass" when the news had spread. The wind was falling and a fog setting in, so that we were long in making the shore, which seemed deserted. Not a curl of smoke went upward from all its length.

Ruth and I stood on the poop, hand in hand, watching that long-desired shore until the fog had thickened and the wind dropped. At this Radisson ordered the anchor put out, and I perforce assisted at the task. When I returned to Ruth she was staring over the rail strangely.

"Davie," she asked in a low voice, "does it not seem to you that the ship is lower in the water this morning?"

"I had not seen it," I replied carelessly. As I looked overside with her my heart leaped up, for in truth the ship was sitting low. I knew that the leak had gained on us, but evidently it was nothing serious, for the men had made no outcry about it.

However, I had scant time to reassure Ruth, for presently Radisson approached us. Grim tagged at his heels, for since my father's illness the dog had taken to following the old man around.

"Davie," he said, "pick out what men can row and get the longboat over. We must make a camp here and relieve the worst cases among the sick, then we can go on to Albany, which I take to be the nearest post."

Save for scattered cakes, the bay was free enough of ice, but the fog now had almost hid the shore from sight. Only three of the crew were able to row—Black Michael, Gib and the sailor Eoghan. That made the four of us, however, and we made shift to get the longboat over the side, by the help of Radisson and Ruth. It was a sad and terrible sight, to watch those others, who had been strong men all, lying about the decks or gazing on us with a wild stare of hope.

When the boat was over, we began lading her as our captain ordered us, with canvas, stores, powder, fusils and a host of other things.

"We will set out a camp," declared Radisson, when at length the boat was laden to the gunwales. "Then the sick will go on shore while I gather herbs and green things which I know well. With these, we will be enabled to overcome the scurvy in a few days, I trust."

What might have passed for a feeble cheer went up from the pathetic group above us, but even as Radisson leaped down into the boat, Eoghan went forward over his oar with a single groan. I tried to pull him up, but the poor fellow could not move. The scurvy had taken hold on him of a sudden, and he muttered that his joints were aflame. Radisson would have taken his place, but with a flash Ruth was over the rail and had pushed him away.

"I can row as well as you," she laughed. "Save your strength, sir! Yours is of more worth to us than is mine."

"Aye, let the lassie go!" And with amazement I beheld my father clinging to the rail above and staring down with ghastly eyes. "God speed your errand and give you His blessing!" Methought he spoke more to me than Radisson, and later this reflection has comforted me, for this was the last word I ever had with my father Fergus.

So Radisson nodded to Ruth and we pushed away from the ship. Then for the first time I noticed that Grim had followed us into the boat and was crouched in the stern beside the old white-haired wanderer. Over us gathered the other dogs, and the last token we had as we pulled away into the fog was the full-throated bark of Tam Graham's Sandy.

There was no wind and the fog lay thick and wet about us. Ahead rose the gray line of the shore, grim enough for all its touch of green. As I looked back at the ship I realized more than ever the truth behind those words of Homer, beaten into my head by my father—" Let us go up the sounding seas!" For the water seemed to rise behind until they met and blended with the gray wall of mist above; and in the midst, dim and ghostly, hung the "Lass o' Dee." That picture clung long in my memory—that, and the brown shoulders of Gib o' Clarclach rising and falling before me on the after-thwart.

Presently Radisson cried to us to cease rowing, and I glanced over my shoulder to see a line of black rocks a few yards away. Black Michael, in the bow, fended us in and sprang ashore with a shout of rejoicing which we all echoed as we followed him, even Grim catching the enthusiasm and giving vent to a series of loud barks.

Bleak rocks lay before and about us, interspersed with small trees and bushes. To one side a little cascading brook trickled down over the rocks into the sea with a quiet murmur. But there was no sign of human life within our limited range of vision.

We were all chilled to the bone by that heavy, dank fog, which by now had closed in thicker than ever, so that when Radisson said he would start a fire we began unloading the boat with alacrity. He disappeared into the bushes, soon emerging with an armful of sticks and bark. By means of my flint and steel we soon had a fire blazing, dragged poor Eoghan up from the boat, and clustered joyfully about the warmth.

"David," said Radisson after a little, "do you and your sister come with me. We must see to curing this scurvy, which I fear is getting into my old bones at last."

Catching Ruth's hand I pulled her up with a laugh and we left Black Michael and Gib staring at us dully, across the half-senseless body of Eoghan.

"Wait, lad," Radisson pointed to a clump of bushes. "Do you stop here within sight of the camp. In this fog it were an easy matter to get lost beyond repair. Call to us every few moments and pluck all these leaves you can carry. Chew some of them well, while Ruth and I go on after others."

I fell to work on the bushes, cramming my mouth full of the leaves and stuffing my pockets with them. I did not neglect to call out frequently, Ruth's silvery voice rising clearly in response. Meanwhile I carried some of the leaves to the men in camp, and much to my surprise saw Gib o' Clarclach just giving some to Black Michael, so I merely thrust a few into Eoghan's mouth and bade him chew for his life. It was plain that Gib had small need of Radisson's services in this land.

In no great while Ruth and the old man rejoined us, laden down with roots and leaves of divers shapes. These we bruised between stones and with them filled a kettle which had been fetched from the ship. To this was put water, and the kettle was then set over the fire.

"Now," ordered Radisson, "do you stay here, Mistress Ruth, while we go fetch a load of the sick. Keep this brew simmering, so it may be ready on our return."

We stepped toward the boat, but Gib and Black Michael made no move to arise. Radisson spoke to them sharply, whereat Gib growled sullenly in French.

"Do the work yourself, an' you will! I be not going to budge from solid earth for you or—"

He got no farther, for Radisson took one long step to his side, his stern old face livid with sudden fury. Seizing the man by the throat, he lifted him with one hand and dashed him back to the ground, like as I have seen my father dash a spider from him.

"Obey me, you dog! Get to the boat, both of yon, lest I forget myself!"

Coming from the old man of seventy, the words may seem ludicrous enough; but there was that in his voice which brought the two men to their feet without a word more. Sullenly they stepped into the boat while Radisson watched them. Then he turned to me.

"In with you. Davie! We'll leave Ruth to take care of Eoghan."

"Willingly," she laughed gaily, then added more soberly, "You'll bring father back in the first boat, Davie?"

"That we will, lass." I made hearty answer, and she watched us off, her hand resting on Grim's head. The ship was hid from us in the fog, but Radisson had her compass-bearing from the shore. Now there happened a fearsome thing, a thing which has made my blood run chill many a night since.

Just before the shore was closed from sight, I saw Grim lift his head from Ruth's hand and utter one long howl. So mournful was that voice, so terrible in the loneliness around, that it drew a curse from Black Michael, and I shivered despite myself. And in this same moment came another howl—but now from the fog ahead of us—a long deep cry which I recognized for old Sandy's, and it was cut short in the midst as by his master's hand. But Tam Graham was lying sick between decks, as we well knew.

And with that I felt that something was wrong. I believe that we all sensed it, for the others fell to their oars and Radisson's shaggy white brows drew far down. Knowing Grim as I did, I was far more fearful than the others; only once before had I heard such sound from his throat, and that was on the day my mother died.

So as I pulled I cast glances over my shoulder, seeking the ship, and sudden remembrance of Ruth's words that morning put haste, into my oar. My mind was full of its uneasy fear, and it was full five minutes before I realized that we should have come to the ship ere this. I could see naught of her in the fog, and when I looked to Radisson I saw him studying his compass and peering about.

"Have we lost the 'Lass?'" I cried between strokes.

"Strange!" he muttered, frowning. "I had her bearings right enough, but—"

Black Michael cried out in Gaelic that we were of a surety bewitched, and for a moment my heart failed me and I stared at Radisson in horror.

"Her cable was not strong," spoke up Gib, who had lost his surliness of a sudden. "Mayhap it parted and sent her adrift."

"There is no wind to drift her," answered Radisson, perplexed. "Yet we heard the dogs howl plain enough. What make you of it, Davie?"

"God knows!" I half sobbed, staring back over my shoulder in the shuddering fog, that seemed to stifle us, so thick was it. An old word came into my head, and out I blurted it. "Ill's the wind when dogs howl."

At this Black Michael uttered a savage Gaelic oath that was half pure fear, and paused on his oar. For a little we drifted thus, the sullen seas heaving beneath us, driving us slowly up and down yet giving us no sign of what lay beyond that curtain of gray. It was uncanny, and I shivered again until my oar was all but lost.

"Give me that fusil," commanded Radisson. I took up the gun, which was ready loaded, and passed it to him. Lifting it, he fired in the air. There was no answer save a dull echo and the lap-lap of water on our sides. Black Michael went gray with sheer fright.

"Strange," exclaimed Radisson again, and even his deep voice was shaken. "What think you of it, Jean?"

I remembered later how then he turned to the man he hated above all others, and I respected him the more for it. Gib, for it was he whom Radisson addressed, leaned over and snatched something from the water.

"This, Sieur Radisson."

He held up a dripping object. We all stared at it, then I felt my heart leap, and I uttered a cry of horror—for the thing was the front cover of my father's Bible!

CHAPTER VIII

DESERTED

EVEN THAT hardened villain Gib was shocked at this discovery. He handed the soaked leather cover to me in silence, and when I raised my face I saw Radisson gazing at me, a great sadness in his eyes. I stammered out what the thing was, and thereafter silence fell upon us all.

I knew full well that some dire thing had happened before that sacred Bible could have been wrenched asunder in my father's hands, for seldom indeed had it ever left him. I stood up on the seat and shotted in a frenzy of fear, for that horrible fog set badly on my soul.

"Father! Father! Where are you?"

But through the mist came only one faint reply—a weird howl from the throat of Grim. I sank back staring and Radisson gave a short order.

"Pull, all of you! Somewhat has happened to the ship, plain enough. Yet may we rescue some of the poor souls aboard her, if it be God's will."

We gave way with desperate energy, but though we rowed back and forth in that blanketed fog for nigh an hour, we found no sign of Wat Herries' ship other than the torn, watersoaked fragment of leather that lay in my shirt bosom. Despair sat heavily upon us all, and at length Radisson, his face haggard and terrible, swept us about and we gave up the vain search.

It must be that the touch of scurvy and the hardships of that voyage had sapped my strength, and that this horrible day had

set a finish upon it, for I remember nothing more save staggering to the camp, when we had reached the shore, and meeting
Ruth as she advanced. Then I fell forward, my arms going about
Grim's shaggy neck; I tried to sob out something, and therewith
fainted dead away.

I recovered to find Ruth feeding me a bitter herb-brew, which
I pushed from me as I sat up. My head had been in her arms,
and when my eyes met hers I remembered all, and near cried
out but with the shock of the memory. For the grief in her sweet
face showed all too clearly that she had been told of the tidings.
Then Grim licked my hand, whereat I rose to my feet; it came
to me in that instant that there was a new burden now on my
shoulders, and that I must show myself for a man indeed.

"Here, Davie," cried out Radisson, "come and help me with
this canvas. Ruth, give Eoghan some more of that brew."

I joined him and the other two, and under his guidance we
stretched the canvas into some semblance of a tent that would
make a rude shelter for us. When this had been done to his
liking, Radisson had us rear, a little distance off, a shedlike cover
of boughs over which he flung our plaids. This was for the use
of Ruth.

"Come, lad," and a heavy hand fell on my shoulder. "No more
of this staring into the fog-cloud; help us gather firewood
against the night."

Turning, I looked into the face of Black Michael and recognized his rough but kindly attempt to hearten me. I had not
thought it of him, so dark and sullen the man was ever, and the
memory of those few words has always touched him kindly in
my mind. So I helped him gather wood, after which we made
a sorry enough meal, our first in the New World.

Eoghan was somewhat recovered by now, and the leaves and
brew had done us all good, even in that little time. But none
the less we were in desperate case, and our gathering was a quiet
one. When the meal was done Radisson beckoned me to one
side.

"Come you for a little exploring, David."

But when we had left the camp and were among the trees, his tone changed and he gripped me by the shoulder, whirling fiercely upon me.

"Lad, there be three fusils and five horns of powder yonder in the camp. Get them all safe stowed away in hiding, for we may have trouble from these men ere long."

I stared at him agape. "Why, do you fear—"

"Obey orders!" he snapped. Then, his face relaxing from its anxious tensity, he continued more kindly. "Aye, I fear that for one thing the ship is lost, David. When this cursed fog lifts we shall know for certain; but hope for little. I misdoubt that great howl from the dogs; besides, there was no answer to our cries or shot. All those aboard her were too weak to man the pumps, and I fear she has filled and gone down at her anchor."

I was about to make reply when he checked me.

"We have ourselves to depend on, David. Brace up, lad—remember that your sister must be saved by us."

"Saved—from what?" I repeated. "We have the boat and can make our way—"

"Peace," he cried. "You know nothing of the dangers about us, even in our own party. Do my bidding in the matter of the fusils and powder. Say as little as may be to anyone, especially to Ruth, for I may be wrong and it were not well to alarm her. Go now—I will return presently."

So in no little alarm and perplexity I returned, to find no change in affairs at the camp. The three fusils and the powder were easily secured and I placed them in Ruth's shelter in charge of Grim. The weather remained as it had been, the fog still heavy on the waters.

Side by side, Ruth and I sat near the fire for hours. In truth, the poor maid was drooping with sheer fatigue. I, poor lout, could think of naught cheering to say to her, and so we sat and listened to the lapping of the waves below and the chance talk of the three men. I mentioned it not to Ruth, but the more I saw of Gib the more I feared and hated the fellow, though for no very tangible reason save the words of Radisson. And those I understood but dimly for many days to come.

Toward the sunset Radisson returned to us, bearing two dead rabbits. These were prepared and Ruth cooked them, giving us a wholesome change from the salt meat. Gradually the darkness fell, and we built up the fire until its warmth gave us such a glow as we had not known for weeks.

That night Radisson told us many stories of his adventures in this very country and in the Canadas to the south. He told how he had been captured as a lad by the Mohawk Indians and how he had finally become a great man among them, before returning to his own people. Then he told of that great empire of the redmen, called the Five Nations, of which the Mohawks are the greatest; of his later travels in the west and of how he had discovered that great river called "Father of Waters" by the Indians, which in later days had been "discovered" anew, for Radisson never stood well with the Papists. To his stories the men listened eagerly, Gib with a half sneer, but little did I heed their glumness. Ruth and I forgot ourselves in Radisson's words, which was perhaps as he had intended.

So drew that day to a close. Seldom in my life have I known a more terrible one—not from its actual danger, but from the mere lawfulness of the unknown. Only once have I felt greater terror, and of that you shall hear in its proper place.

In the night a little breeze arose. I woke once to find Radisson building the fire anew, and cast my eyes toward the star-hung waters. But no ship's light could I see, and I think I sobbed myself to sleep in misery of heart, for I remember Gib cursing me in some strange tongue.

With the morning our worst fears were confirmed. There before us lay the blue bay glittering in the sun, but never a sign of the "Lass o' Dee." To north and west the shore stretched, while the country behind us seemed thickly wooded and deserted. It was a strange thing, to me at least, to see all that land with not a single spiral of smoke curling up from any farm or stead.

That the ship had sunk with all on board, I no longer had any doubt. Fortunately, we had good store of provisions, and as I sat with Ruth that morning and gazed out across the water, I did my best to cheer up the poor maid. The loss of my father and the rest was a great shock to her, coming as it had, but she was never much given to grieving and sat there dry-eyed. Pretty enough she looked, despite her grief, for her yellow hair fell braided over her shoulders and her great violet eyes stared out from beneath her fine, high brows. Looking at her in this moment, I was startled by a likeness of her profile to that of old Radisson; howbeit, I said nothing of it at the time.

No sooner had we made sure of the ship's loss than Radisson vanished with one of the fusils, and after a time we heard a faint shot. The men were already like new, the scurvy symptoms vanishing rapidly before the herb-brew and roots, and I myself could feel the great change which these had worked in me.

Slowly the morning drew on, and then Radisson appeared bearing parts of a deer-like animal he called a caribou. When we had eaten and drunk we felt wondrous better, both in body and mind.

"It is hard to realize," said Ruth very soberly, "that we alone are left alive out of all that ship's company. It seems like some evil dream."

"It is no dream, maid," returned Radisson sadly, "but cold reality. It behooves us to make some plan, my friends. Where think you we are, Jean?"

And now for the second time Gib answered to the French name. Truly, he seemed a person of many titles.

"I would say to the northwest of Albany," he replied slowly, cocking his evil face up at the sky. "The southern shore is lower than this, methinks. We might be near those barren lands the Chippewas tell of."

"Down with the gun, lad. These be friends."

Radisson nodded. "So it seemed to me, although I have never been up through these more northern lands. Then our best plan will be to go south in the boat. Surely we ought to reach the fort within a day or so, and then—"

Radisson paused suddenly. I saw the eyes of Gib grow small and cold and hard, and they met those of the old wanderer insolently.

"And then?" He repeated half mockingly, with a triumphant leer. "England and France are at peace, in these parts! And perchance the Governor would pay as well for a certain hostage we wot of as would certain parties in New France."

Radisson said nothing, but looked at the man steadily for a long while, though I saw the cords of his neck bulge out. At length the bold eyes of Gib shifted and then fell beneath that intent look, and our leader spoke calmly and quietly.

"I think we will all be able to row in the morning. We will start then. If need be, we can make a sail of this canvas. This afternoon we will reload the boat."

Now it seemed to me that a single swift glance passed between Gib and Black Michael. Then the latter wagged his great beard dubiously.

"I fear me we are in no great spirit for rowing. Master Radisson," he grumbled, although an hour before lie had been working well enough over the fire. "My joints are sore, and Eoghan here can barely move."

"Fool, to take Pierre Radisson for a child!" That was all the old man said, but before his eyes Black Michael seemed to shrink back in confused silence. If this kept on, I knew that Radisson would be goaded into action we might all regret; albeit, boylike. I rejoiced thereat as the thought came to me. Then I fell to pondering on that puzzle which had vexed me so sore—Gib o' Clarclach. Who was he? Had Radisson told me truly or no? And who was this hostage of whom he had spoken? But I knew no more at the end of that pondering than I knew at the beginning.

During the afternoon we loaded most of our goods back into the boat, so that in the morning we might make a start. Most of the provisions were put aboard, together with the spare clothes and other things we had fetched from the ship, but the fusils, powder and shot I left where they had been hid. And fortunate it was that I did so, as events fell out.

To tell the truth, I think Ruth grieved more for my father than did I. He had ever been a hard man, just but stern in all things, and I had been more my mother's son while she lived. The thing was rather a shock than a heart-grief to me. I verily believe, and bitterly have I reproached myself that it was so, but without avail.

That night I noticed that Black Michael cast anxious glances at us, and the sailor Eoghan stared more than once at the gold brooch at Ruth's throat. I thought long on this, and it brought again to my mind that scene on the beach near Rathesby, when Gib and the other had fallen to staring at the brooch also. What might the thing be, and whose arms were those graven upon it? But this Ruth knew as little as I, and I concluded that the men were but attracted by the glitter of the massy gold, as was like enough.

This night fell warm and clear, very different from that before. Now Radisson and I lay together, the other three sleeping beyond us and nearer to the fire. I wrapped my plaid about me, as I had done many a time on the moors at home, and fell asleep almost at once; as yet I was none too strong, and even the little work done that day had wearied me. Grim lay beside Ruth's shelter.

How long I slept I know not, but when I wakened the fire had died down to a red glow. I lay wondering what had roused me, then sat up. The place where Gib had lain was vacant.

But I was too sleepy to waste time on such little things, and so rolled over again and dropped off. When next I opened mine eyes it was to find Radisson bending over and shaking me roughly.

"Waken. David!" Something in that deep rich voice of his brought me to my feet.

"What is it?" I cried, staring about into the new dawn. "What is the matter?"

"Matter enough," replied the old man gravely. "The men have gone off with the boat, lad, and we are deserted!"

CHAPTER IX

THE GREAT ADVENTURE BEGINS

I LOOKED AROUND, dazed. Of the three men there was no sign, and the boat was gone from the shore. As I stared, scarce believing mine own eyes, Ruth and Grim came toward us. The lassie had heard the news already, for at my exclamation of anger she tried to hearten us with a laugh, and slipped her hand into that of Radisson.

"Never mind, Davie, we are better off without them! So put that black look from your face and let them go, since they will have it so; they will only fetch us succor the sooner."

Radisson but grunted—a habit he had when words failed him.

"The cowards!" I broke forth hotly, staring across the vacant waters. " 'Tis little we can look to them for, Ruth. To steal off and leave us in our sleep!" And I told how I had awakened during the night.

"You know not the danger, either of you." Radisson shook his head gloomily, the while his fine eyes searched the woods about us. "We must pack what we can carry on our backs. It may be that we shall yet reach the post in safety before them."

I saw no reason why we must hasten to reach the fort ahead of the scoundrels, but at the time it seemed too small a matter to call for exposition. Our leader was no man to bide inactive. We had each a fusil, and good store of powder and shot, while food was to be had for the getting, it seemed. I began to think that this land might not be so barren after all.

64

What was left to us we made into two bundles, Radisson taking one and I the other. Then we set off along the brook, inland. The country was high and bare, save for bushes and evergreen trees, but of heather I saw none; indeed, as I learned later, there was none of our proper heather in all this New World.

As Radisson believed Fort Albany to be toward the southeast, our best plan was to follow the course of the streamlet, which turned from the shore toward the south. We were soon lost in the tangle of bush, and about noon left the stream altogether. Then it developed that the three deserters had taken Radisson's compass; but of this our leader recked little, for he guided us by some sixth sense which he averred was part of the Indian training.

Despite the rough ground and our loads, we must have made full ten or twelve miles that day, and with nightfall camped beside a river of goodly size, making our dinner from a hare which Grim fetched in. It was late before I could sleep, the woods around being filled with strange noises and the calls of birds and animals. In the morning I had my first sight of the men of the New World.

I was about building a fire, on a big rock by the river's edge, when I heard a voice from the water. Looking up, I saw three canoes poised noiselessly in the stream, each bearing two dark-skinned men whose hair hung in braids and who were naked to the waist. Their faces were not painted, as in Radisson's stories, and all were staring at me as at some wondrous marvel.

I cried out and sprang for a fusil, but the paddles swept down once, and even as Radisson awoke the first Indian leaped ashore. I was trying to load a fusil in haste, but Radisson sprang up and halted me after a quick look at the red men.

"Down with the gun, lad. These be friends."

All six of them landed now, but stopped their advance with a gutteral word of surprise at sight of the old wanderer. I laid my hand on Grim's bristling neck.

"What cheer!" said Radisson in English. "Has Soan-ge-ta-ha forgotten his friend the White Eagle?"

One of the Indians, older than the rest, gravely took the extended hand of Radisson and made reply in very good English, to my surprise.

"Brave Heart has not forgotten the Eagle, although his young men know him not, and the winters have left their snows on his hair. Will the Eagle and his children go to the post with us?"

At this Radisson broke into a strange tongue and I could make nothing of the talk that ensued. Ruth had come to my side and was watching the red men somewhat fearfully, while in their turn they bestowed open admiration upon her. Soon they came forward and bunched around the fire while they talked. After a little Radisson turned to me, and spoke rapidly, in French.

"Davie, these be men of the Chippewa nation, who will take us to the fort. On your life speak not in English of Gib!"

While I was puzzling over this command, Ruth had turned to the speaker.

"But why do you go thither?" she asked anxiously. "Surely you could send us with—"

"Nay, daughter," replied the old wanderer, "these are not to be trusted, although they fear to deceive or harm me. Say no more, for we go to the post."

He drew a deep breath, then took one of our fusils and presented it to the chief, Brave Heart. The gift was received with a murmur of joy, and although I could make nothing of the words, the eyes of the six Indians betrayed the fierce delight in their hearts at the gift. But there was no gratitude mingled with that delight, and as they sat and eyed the gift methought I could see the murder-lust in their glances. It has always seemed to me that the Adventurers to whose post we were going, have done little good; for in all that land north of New France they have but taught the red men to slay and slay for skins, and mingled little enough of the word of God with the word of man. Howbeit, to my story.

It is not my purpose to detail the strange customs and sights which Ruth and I saw during the next few days and nights while we paddled up that river. To others they might not seem so strange as they did to us, and moreover I have greater things to tell of which befell later. Soan-ge-ta-ha, or Brave Heart, had known Radisson both as friend and foe, years before, and very plainly held the old man in vast respect and fear.

For two days we ascended the river, then came a portage where the canoes and furs were carried for a mile or more to another stream, which we descended this time. On the third day we met another party of four natives, also Chippewas, who exchanged words with Brave Heart, greeted us with a mingling of fear and awe, and pushed on ahead.

"They cannot understand it," laughed Radisson in French, which these others knew not. "They have seen no ship along the coast and are beginning to think the Great Spirit dropped us here from the sky."

I marveled at the credulity of the poor creatures, and suggested that it was wrong so to deceive them, whereat Radisson looked queerly at me. As Ruth failed to agree, I dropped the subject for the time, although I liked not to continue in such standing, which to my mind savored of deceit and well-nigh blasphemy. By this you may see that I was no little changed from the young lout who had slipped out of the Purple Heather at Rathesby to skip the prayers—as well I might be, after the horror of that voyage and its ending.

We traveled each in a separate canoe, seeing little of each other save at the halting places. On one of these occasions Radisson told me why he had ordered no mention made of Gib. It seemed that the fellow was of no little reputation among the Chippewas, even as was Radisson among other tribes, and if his return to the New World were known things might go ill.

Ruth made light of the hardships of those first days, although Brave Heart's men treated her with all consideration. Both she and I gained some slight knowledge of the art of paddling, and I found that the scurvy had altogether disappeared, whereat I thanked God most fervently.

It seemed that the Chippewa chief, Soan-ge-ta-ha, was one of the greatest among his own people. He was not so old as Radisson, but his face held a stern, implacable aspect which at times set me athrill with fear of the man. I prayed that we might never have him to face as an enemy, nor at that time did such an event seem probable.

And as we paddled I grew ever more amazed at the great size of this new land, which seemed to have neither limit nor end. On we went, crossing from one stream to another. We had been with the six Chippewas for eight days, and on the fifth day after meeting the four others Soan-ge-ta-ha announced the post was only three days' journey off. Of this we were right glad, and if Radisson felt in any other wise he gave no sign.

But we were not destined to accompany the six farther, for here happened one of those wonderful things which showed ever more plainly that the hand of God was over us, guiding and protecting us from hidden dangers. We had just made ready to embark when Soan-ge-ta-ha lifted his hand in a warning gesture, and Grim gave a low growl. As he did so, the bushes on the farther side of our camping-place parted, and out stepped two men.

But what men they were! Ruth gave a little cry and settled back within my arm, while the Chippewas emitted a grunt of surprise. Both the men were Indians—just such savages as Radisson had described to us while on the "Lass." Naked to the waist like our own six, the face and breast of each was hideously painted with red and white paint, and they wore pantaloons of skin, beaded and fringed wondrously. Each was taller than the average man, and their heads were in part shaven so that a single long lock of hair was left, and in this were twisted eagle feathers. As they came closer I saw that for all their sturdiness these were old men, in years if not in vigor. They carried no muskets, but at their belts were hatchets and knives. For an instant we all stared as if rooted to the ground, then to my utter amazement Radisson leaped forward and threw his arms about the first savage.

"My brother—my brother!" he cried out in French, all his heart in his voice. "Am I dreaming or bewitched? Can this thing be possible?" He turned and caught the other likewise. "And you, Swift Arrow—is it you or some ghost of the olden days?"

As if this were not surprise enough for me, these grave painted savages of the New World made dignified response in French. Nay, it was poor French enough, yet Ruth and I could sense it with ease.

"Now are we indeed happy," spoke the older of the two, paying no heed to us who watched in amazement. "My brother, many snows ago you left us. We heard that you had gone to the Great Father across the big water. Then it was borne to us that you were far in the north, here among the snows.

"My brother, our lodges were empty. We mourned for you in the Long House among the Nations. There was no war among us and we grew old. So we bade our people farewell and left the land of the Long House to seek you. My brother, we have found you, and we thank the Great Spirit. We, who were young together, shall grow old together and travel the Ghost-trail together. I, Ta-cha-noon-tia the Black Prince, Keeper of the Eastern Door, have said it."

For an instant there was a tense silence. I did not realize what the speech portended, but I could see Radisson's face, and I watched it glow in the morning sun until it seemed as if youth had once more touched it lightly for an instant, so glorified was it. Then Soan-ge-ta-ha made a step forward, for he knew no French.

"Who are these?" he asked, sweeping a hand toward the strangers with a frown. "What do they in the country of the Chippewas?"

The pair seemed to sense the spirit of the words if not their meaning, for they drew themselves up proudly and topped the Chippewas by a head. It was Radisson who made hasty answer.

"These are brothers of mine from the far south, Brave Heart. They came in search of me, and are on no war trail." He turned and addressed the two in a strange, gutteral tongue. They made answer with a few gestures. I saw Radisson cast a quick look at me; there was that in his face which spelled danger. Therewith he turned to the Chippewas again.

"Soan-ge-ta-ha has been generous to his friends, as befits a great chief, and we thank him. Let him keep our gifts in token of friendship, for we may go no farther with him. We depart from this place with these my brothers."

The Chippewas glanced at the two impassive figures, and there was greed in their eyes as they took in the exquisite garments, the fine weapons, the—ah, what was that dark line fringing the belts? Radisson had told me of the strange custom of wearing an enemy's hair, and I turned away my eyes as I recognized only too plainly the scalps that fringed the girdles of these two old strangers.

Soan-ge-ta-ha eyed Radisson for an instant. Perhaps he had a conflicting mind, but if so he thought better of it, for he only nodded and spoke briefly to his warriors. These, without a word to us, leaped into the loaded canoes, and with a last wave from the chief the six pushed off into the stream.

"What did he say?" spoke up Ruth hurriedly. "Why is this? Be these men going to take us to the post?"

Radisson came and took her hand, speaking in English.

"My child, these men have done what few had dared attempt—they have come here from below the Canadas, far to the south, in search of me. They belong to the Mohawk nation, the greatest tribe of the Iroquois, and long ago I lived with them and loved them. Ruth, these are two great men in their own land, famous both of them—they—they—"

Here his emotion choked him, for he turned his face away and I saw a tear upon his white beard. After a moment he caught my hand with Ruth's and turned about. Now he spoke in French.

"Ta-cha-noon-tia, Black Prince, you who ward the Eastern Door of the Long House of the Five Nations, and you, Ca-yen-gui-nano. Great Swift Arrow, I give into your friendship and protection this young man, who is as mine own son, and this girl, who is the daughter of mine own sister."

And at that Ruth gave a great cry and caught Radisson by the hands, staring at him wildly.

CHAPTER X

THE KEEPER AND THE ARROW

"**WHAT MEAN** you?" she broke forth, searching his smiling face. Is this a jest, sir? Or do you really know—"

"My child," and Radisson caught her to him, touching her brow with his lips, "it is no jest. But we are in grave danger here. Come, greet these noblest of men, and let us begone. The tale I will give you in full at the first chance."

Both the two Mohawks and I had looked on at this scene with no little bewilderment. But as Ruth obeyed him and turned to them with a puzzled smile, the elder, whom we came to know as the Keeper, stepped forward and caught her band to his lips in right courtly fashion—doubtless learned at Montreal.

"The Yellow Lily need fear not, for we are brothers of the White Eagle," and he glanced at Radisson, then turned to me. His black eyes glittered intensely as they swept over me, but it was his companion, the Arrow, who spoke. Doubtless he put his Mohawk thought into French speech, for the words were abrupt.

"The young man with brave eyes is good to look upon. He is our brother."

"Then we will care for the Yellow Lily together." I smiled at Ruth, using the name they had bestowed upon her. This pleased them hugely, and a smile flickered across their dark faces. Presently they and Radisson were chattering in the strange tongue, and when he turned to us there was doubt in his strong face, for once.

"My children, we are in a narrow path. These twain have lived for two years among the Cree people, daily waiting my coming. But a few days since they had journeyed to the post. Gib, Eoghan and Black Michael had arrived in the boat. No sooner was their story told than men were sent out in all directions in search of us, while among the Chippewas a price was set on our heads in beads and blankets.

"What!" I cried indignantly. "Would they dare—"

"Peace, lad. You know not all the tale, and it is too long to be told here. There is no law in these parts save that of the strongest, and the Keeper and the Arrow set forth to find us. Fortunately, Soan-ge-ta-ha had not heard the news, else he had not let us go so easily. As I will explain later, it is impossible for Ruth to seek the post. The only thing left us is to go with my friends here and find refuge among the Crees to the west. There we shall be safe, for the Crees are old friends of mine. The Mohawks have two canoes hidden a few miles from here. Let us go on with them, and we can take to the water on another river. This will throw off any pursuers until we can find shelter among friends."

"I glanced at Ruth, despair in my eyes. She read the look and came to me, putting her hand on my arm.

"Davie, dear, there is naught else to do. Have no fear for me, but let us trust in God. Remember, we have much to talk of and we do not know all that has passed. Are you willing to go into the wilderness with us?"

"Willing?" I burst out, seizing her hand. "Aye, for myself I care naught, Ruth, but for you—is there no other way?"

"There is no other way, my son," returned Radisson gravely.

"Then let us go forth and seek what may betide," I answered bitterly.

There was no time lost. Our few belongings were all ready, and we set out after Radisson who followed in the steps of the

Keeper. As for the Arrow, he melted into the bushes and was gone—to scout for danger and to meet us at the canoes, explained the old wanderer.

That march through the forest was one of no little hardship for all of us, but more especially for Ruth and me. There was danger all about us, for at any moment we might come upon parties of Chippewas who were even then searching the forest for trace of us. I walked along as one in a maze, and in truth my poor brain was all bewildered.

"What was the meaning of this strange meeting with the two Mohawks? And Radisson's words to them—was Ruth indeed his niece? That was hardly to be credited, methought, for why had he said no word to us before? And in any case, he could know no more of the maid than did I, who had lived all my life beside her. None the less, the matter troubled me.

In point of distance we had not far to go, but the difficulties of the savage forest beset us sorely. Ruth had much ado to prevent her skirts being torn by thorns and jagged branches. At one time we would be pushing through thick-grown saplings, and at another leaping from tussock to tussock of swamp-grass. The Keeper and Radisson, better accustomed to such places, moved like shadows; but had there been any foe near, my crashing must have betrayed our presence beyond a doubt.

Yet all things draw to an end, and the end of our journey was a clear, open lake of good size. Not a hundred yards from where we emerged, The Arrow stood waiting beside the shore, and at his feet were two canoes. Here was a new wonder to me, that the Keeper should have guided us so surely through those track-less woods to the side of his comrade.

But Ruth was fain for rest, and so was I. We sank down beside the canoes, and here Radisson joined us.

"Now," he said with a certain vigor and spring in his voice which was new to me. "I will explain things to you, my children. In the first place, you are verily my sister's daughter, Ruth. It was nigh twenty years ago that I left her in Montreal, new-married to the Sieur de Courbelles, and my last gift to her was that brooch you wear at your throat. See—those are mine own arms upon it! Then I left New France, but she, with her husband, was to join me in London town. I never heard word of her again, my child; there can be no doubt that their ship was driven far north and you alone were saved."

He paused a space, and I saw that Ruth's own little fingers had stolen out to grasp his. But here there came a great light to me.

"Then," I exclaimed, "was that why Gib o' Clarclach was so hasty after Ruth? Nay, but it could hardly have been so, for he had scarce recognized that little brooch!"

"Not that, David," smiled the old man, "but he knew the arms right well, and doubtless he also knew the tale of my sister and her loss by shipwreck. I must tell you, lad, that the man who you know as Gib, whom I know as Jean Lareau, whom the Indians hereabouts know to their cost as The Pike, is an agent of France—a spy, who serves France or England according as he is best paid. No one knows, or ever will know, just who his masters are. So you see, lad, that if he could lay hold on the maid and fetch her to Paris, they might get me into their clutches again right easily."

"But not that!" I exclaimed angrily. "Frenchmen would never dare go to such extremes with a maid of good birth—"

Radisson's face went black. "No? Wait till you know them as I do, the Jesuit dogs! If you want the truth of it, that man Gib is no man of France so much as he is a paid spy of the Order— the Order that has hounded me, stolen the credit of discoveries, sent forth its men in my place to gain mine honor, and at the last tried to steal this child of my blood!"

And therewith he went on to tell me things I had not dreamed possible. He told of his long trips through the wilderness, of how he had found the "Father of Waters," how his reports had been stolen and altered, his furs stolen from him, and how on the strength of his labors the Jesuits had sent out men of their order to take the credit for his work.

"But why?" asked Ruth with wondering eyes. "Why should they do this thing? Surely there are honorable and good men among—"

"Aye, lass, there are," Radisson made quick response. "But the reason for it is simply that I am none of their faith. When a lad I was taken by the Mohawks and grew up among them. Then I returned to mine own people, but I never forgot my adopted nation. On all my trips I carried Iroquois with me. The Arrow here went to the Detroit with me years before the settlement was founded there. The Keeper was behind me when the Sioux people saw their first white face, and when I was led to the great river in the South."

With that our conversation was ended, for The Arrow approached and warned us that the day was drawing on apace. We made a light meal off some dried venison, after which we embarked in the canoes. In one went The Arrow, Ruth and I, while The Keeper and Radisson-embarked in the other, and we followed in their course across the lake to the mouth of a little river that flowed westward.

So it came about that I set my back toward my own people. I sat in the bow, The Arrow in the stern. Whiles we paddled, and whiles floated where the river was more rapid, but Ruth talked ever with us. I could hear her chattering with the stolid man in the stern, who seemed to waken into life at her words, and so we gained some knowledge of these two strange Indians and their ways.

Of the Iroquois confederacy Radisson had already told us much, and of their Long House, which was not unlike the Houses of Parliament in London town. Here the Five Nations sent their delegates to make laws and give judgments, and the highest chief of each nation kept the doors. The Mohawks, who lived farther east than the rest, held the eastern door of that savage parliament, which fact had given the Black Prince his title. I wondered at his name being the same as that of a former prince of England, but the reason therefor I never knew.

As we wended on our way my gloom began to drop from me. I realized how Radisson felt, and the fact that before us lay a great new land where no white man was, thrilled me to the marrow. I drew the good free air deep into my lungs and put away all thought of that villain Gib o' Clarclach; all these plottings were left behind us, and only the open country and friends lay before. What if these friends were red? From the talk of The Arrow, red friends were as good as or better than white.

Since then I have realized more truly just what that terrible journey from the Canadas had meant for the two Mohawks. Alone and unaided they had traversed a wilderness of foes to find the man they loved as brother. When they came to the Cree people they chanced upon traces of him, Radisson being well known to the Crees, and for his sake the strangers had been taken in and provided for. Their prowess soon made them great men among the Crees, whose customs were not so very different, though less bloody; and during the two years they had spent, waiting for Radisson with a firm faith in his coming, their position had been firmly established. All these things came to me not at once, but slowly, during the many days we paddled on, heading toward the west, and then to the north. Our way was slow, because on the third day one of the canoes was ripped on a rock and we had to wait for a hasty patching. The weather was very warm indeed, but cold at night.

So it came about that when pursuit had been left far behind, we were in the Barren Places, as The Keeper named them. And they deserved the name, being of swamp and scrub trees and thickets of saplings; but of game there was plenty. In this place came the danger to Ruth, and here we first encountered the Mighty One, of whom I will have great things to tell in their own place.

One morning Ruth and I had left the camp for an early ramble. I took a fusil, thinking to kill a deer or caribou. We climbed a little hill above the camp and entered the thicker woods, where after a while we became separated, Ruth halting beside some bushes of berries, very good to the taste. I was perhaps a hundred yards from her when I heard a sudden cry.

Whirling about, I saw a wondrous beast plunging toward the lass. Of monstrous build he was, with huge shoulders and head, while great splay-horns added to his frightful mien. In terror, Ruth made shift to get behind a tree, while the monster stood shaking his head and striking the earth with his hoofs.

I had been so startled that for a moment I forgot my fusil. Never had I dreamed of so huge a beast! I shouted at him and ran forward, whereat he came at me speedily. Ruth cried out again, and in mighty fear I raised my weapon, thinking to see fire come from his nostrils at any moment, for I took him as little less than the fiend himself.

But now he had turned again to Ruth, and the little maid was barely keeping the tree between them. In desperation, I poured fresh powder in the pan and aimed again. This time the weapon spoke, and the added powder sent me backward to the ground with the recoil. Those mighty horns seemed to shoot forward and up, the huge body rose in air, and the next I knew was that the terrible beast was standing over me, scraping at me with his horns. Fortunately, they seemed soft, like those of a deer in summer, and I beat frantically at his enormous nose. An instant later I gripped the horns.

With this, the monster lifted his head and me with it. I gave myself up for lost as he pressed me back into a tree, snorting and grunting, but I hung on grimly enough, for I feared the sharp hoofs.

"Run!" I cried to Ruth, whom I could not see. "Run, Ruth!"

I felt my strength going fast. Now the beast had pushed me in through the branches and was striving to grind me against the tree-trunk itself. Vainly did I writhe and twist away, for those huge horns swung and slashed at me, and had they been hard I had died in that moment. As it was, I felt my ribs crushed in, then a terrific pain shot through me, and my grip loosened.

But even as I fell back, a wild yell sounded in my ears, and a blast of powder-smoke swept by my face. The massy horns were gone, and I scraped back against the tree and came to the ground, helpless and broken.

CHAPTER XI

IN THE VILLAGES OF THE CREES

WHAT HAPPENED after that was of little interest to me. I have brief, fitful memories of things that
occurred at intervals, for as I later learned from Ruth, my hurts
were very sore indeed, and more than once they had given me
up for dead. But for The Keeper and for Radisson himself, who
searched through the woods for healing simples and herbs at
each camping-place, I had been in sorry plight.

I mind me of many days of travel, during no small part of
which I was lashed tightly enough to the canoe. At times Ruth's
face would be above me, her fingers sweeping my brow, and at
times Radisson's kindly white beard would bend over me and
his fingers, for all their sinewy strength, were as tender as those
of Ruth.

That was a dour and terrible journey. Even now, as I sit
writing and gazing over the moors that roll upland beyond
Ayrby, I can feel the throbs of pain across my ribs, and the hurt
of the thwart against my back. And in the damp weather the
feeling is no mere imagination, either.

I remember, after many days of flickering lights and shadows,
there came one time when Ruth's tears fell on my cheeks and
irritated me strangely. Perhaps the lass did not know I was
conscious, for I could speak no word. I heard Radisson attempt
to cheer her, and it seemed that he, too, had lost his heartiness.
Then they died away into blackness once more, and the next
memory is of the Crees.

Queer men they were, queer people, moving like the veriest devils through my half-sensed dreams, although they were our firmest friends. Radisson to them was a deity, and the two Mohawks were little less. They were great hunters and fighters, however, and when my mind came back to me somewhat I never lacked for meat and broth, while skins of the richest were ours in plenty.

When I came to learn of the journey, after I had been injured, it was a tale of hardship and suffering—incurred for the most part on my account. To move a helpless man across the wilderness is a task for the mightiest, and our little party had been sore put to it ere a party of the Crees found us and aided us to their villages.

I came to my clear senses one day, at last, to find a great weight lying upon me, and all dark around. I put up my hand to remove the weight and found that it was the skin of some beast, yet I could not so much as lift it. By this I knew I must be very sick and weak, and for a space the knowledge frighted me oddly.

Suddenly light appeared to one side, and I saw I was lying in a conical shelter, like a tent, and that Ruth stood in the doorway. I called to her weakly enough.

"Eh, lassie! Come and help me."

She gave a little cry and dropped on her knees at my side. But she would not take the fur away, whereat I wondered. Nor would she let me talk, but told me of the journey and of where we now were.

To my utter amazement I found that I had been sick, not for days, but for long weeks. It was a good month and more that I had lain in this shelter, in the Cree village, and near two months since we had met the moose. The first snow had come upon the land, and the days and nights were bitter cold.

In the lodge next to mine dwelt Ruth, and beyond that Radisson and the Mohawks. There was a tale to be told of great wonders, of things and beasts and men such as we had never dreamed of in the old days at Ayrby farm. I listened half-be-lieving, and before she had finished dropped into a deep, pleasant sleep.

Through the days that followed I began to adjust myself somewhat to the new life about me. The Crees—dark, dirty men who wore skins—were kind enough and treated me with not only respect but even deference. For some time I was at a loss to account for this. I presently came to understand that I was looked upon as a great man, greater even than the two Mohawks, which surprised me and troubled me no little. It is not right and just that a man should be so treated by his fellows unless he has proved himself greater than they, and the worship of these poor heathen creatures worried me mightily.

Radisson spent long hours with me, talking and explaining the things all around. Our fusils he had carefully oiled and laid aside, for it seemed that the Crees had never heard the sound of a gun, and the time might come when an appeal to their superstition would do wonders.

"But is that right?" I asked doubtfully. "Methinks it would be more Christian in us to help the poor creatures to understand, than to try and shock them into thinking us men of another world."

"Why, so we are," smiled Radisson. "You see, Davie, we are like to be safe for the present, until the deep snows come. Then we can look for trouble. I have sent out runners to the east and south, for it seems to me that the English around the Bay will not rest until they get news of me. The Chippewa nation is always warring against the Crees, and like enough The Pike will lead them. Our friend is a subtle, crafty fellow and will halt at nothing.

"As for your fears in the matter of religion, Davie, you had best forget them. We can live down to their standard, as does The Pike, or up to our standard, as I have ever done. I have no great wish to preach to them, for their faith is good enough, but do you suit yourself in that regard. It may be that God has not brought us here for nothing, and it is far from my thought to thwart His will."

As the time went by I grew stronger, walking about the village on the arm of Ruth and coming to understand more and more the people among whom we were. Having little else to do, I took to learning their tongue from a chief named Uchichak, or The Crane. He was a fine, upright, silent man of good parts, and as I came to speak the language a little, I told him of the true God. But at this he would ever fall silent, gazing into the fire and saying no word, so that I deemed my talk but wasted.

The Keeper and The Arrow were but indifferent Christians, having been converted years before by the French, and their faith was a mixture of heathenism and religion which was strange to see. Once I protested with The Keeper about taking scalps, whereat he silenced me deftly and firmly.

"Brave Eyes"—for such was the name I now bore—"does not know of what he speaks. Here the nations do not war as our nation wars. The Great Spirit has whispered to me that it is right for the white men to do some things, and wrong for the red men to do some things. He has whispered to Uchichak that it is not right for the Crees to take scalps, and they do not. He has whispered to The Keeper that it is right, and so The Keeper does. He has whispered to the white men that they shall drink of the water of fire. He has whispered to The Keeper not to drink. The Keeper has seen his brothers disobey, and drink, until their minds were stolen from their bodies. The Keeper does not disobey the Great Spirit. Let my brother listen to the Great Spirit, unless he thinks himself greater. Does my brother know more than the Great Spirit?"

It was the longest speech I ever heard from The Keeper, and his quiet sarcasm at the close taught me a lesson that I sorely needed. I had considered myself above these poor heathen people, and in time I came to know that in many ways I was below them. We did not worship alike, yet we all worshiped. There was much that they could and did teach me, and Uchichak came to be a very good friend to me.

The two Mohawks came to rather disregard me and Ruth, centering themselves on Radisson alone, quietly but insistently. They hunted and fished with him, or alone, and left me to Uchichak, who proved an able teacher. Those were happy weeks for me, as I slowly came back to strength and health, and I believe that never in her life had Ruth been so filled with the joy of youth as she was here. And it was well, for there were dark days to come.

As to our future, that was unsettled. Radisson was filled with a great dream of going on into the sunset and searching out the country there, of finding lands where no white man had ever trod. His age was as nothing to him, and I verily believe that except for Ruth he had departed long since. But the love of the little maid restrained him, and his great vision waited on her will.

With the snows, I set forth on the heels of Uchichak, learning to hunt and fish and trap as did the Crees. Our fusils and little store of powder were jealously guarded away, so that perforce I had to 'earn the bow and spear. I learned that moose and elk and bison were no creatures from the nether world, but animals of flesh and blood, and one day I proposed to The Crane that we should seek out the moose who had attacked us, and who had so nearly killed me. At the suggestion a strange expression swept across the chief's dark, handsome face, and he glanced at me with a worried look.

"Is my brother so anxious to meet the Great Spirit? Has he not escaped the horns of the Mighty One by a-miracle?"

"Nonsense!" I retorted. "The Great Spirit did not give me the heart of a coward, Uchichak. He saved me from the moose, and if it be His will, I shall some day meet and slay the animal. Why do you call him the Mighty One?"

It seemed to me that The Crane fell to trembling, almost. Certainly his face quivered, and he glanced around uneasily. We stood alone, our snowshoes leaving a faint trail across a bare rise of snow, carrying a small deer between us. The chief set down his end of the pole and faced me.

"You have said many things to me that I do not understand, my brother. You have told me of the Great Spirit whom you serve, and sometimes I have thought that He was our own Great Spirit also. You have told me how He came to your people and let men kill Him, which to me seemed very foolish, so that I knew He was not the same Great Spirit."

In that moment I saw the mistake I had made. I had told Uchichak the bare story of the Gospels, but had not explained that story. There, standing in the snow beside the stiff and frozen deer, with his intent gaze fixed on me, I spoke as best I might. Indeed, the words seemed to come to me as if placed in my mouth, and when I had made an end I knew not what I had said.

But Uchichak gazed at me silently, and I think that he had understood the greater part of my speech, for I had spoken mostly in his own tongue, haltingly but simply enough that a child might understand.

"You have spoken well, my brother," he returned slowly. "I have understood your words, although your speech is harsh, and it seemed to me that not you were speaking, but the Great Spirit whom yon worship. Listen. It is well that my people should hear of this also. We are not like the Sioux or the Chippewas, blind to all things. We are eager to let our ears be open, and our old men are very wise. To-morrow night shall a Council be held, and before the Council you shall tell these things."

Without pausing for answer, he stooped and we picked up the deer. Our way home was silent enough, and I dared to dream that I had impressed The Crane with some knowledge of the true God. But this was far from the case, as I was to learn.

I have passed over lightly my days of striving, when I was learning to live this new life, for of late my fingers have grown somewhat stiff and the quill hard to hold, and I have that to tell of which must not be delayed. At this time the winter was well onward, and many of the men were away from the village, hunting in the Barren Places. Of Gib and his Chippewas we had heard nothing.

"Grim, all this time, had remained close to me and Ruth. The Indian dogs, used for hauling sleds in winter, seemed idle, frivolous creatures to him, and he disdained to give them attention. The Crees were inclined to sneer at him as a "lodge-dog," good for nothing except to lie beside the fire, until one day two of their fighting brutes went for him. Grim, forced to the combat, made such short work of the wolf-like beasts that thereafter the others slunk past him in fear, while the Crees also gave him a wide berth.

Upon reaching the village that night, we found that Radisson and the Mohawks had left for a two-day elk hunt. A little dismayed at their absence, I sought out Ruth and told her of my conversation with the chief.

"We will face them together, Davie," she said softly, her deep eyes aglow. "A woman is not admitted to the council, yet Uchichak can persuade them easily enough. They are not stern, fierce people like the Mohawks, and they will listen to me."

Gladly enough I asked Uchichak. After a moment he nodded gravely.

"She may speak, and then go. It is not permitted that women should sit in the council."

This was the best I could get out of him, but it was enough. There was no sign of Radisson the next afternoon, and as the council-lodge was made ready I began to miss his support. Ruth and I knew that we would have no great ordeal before us, but it would be hard indeed to break through the stolidity of the Crees, to appeal to their finer feelings. That they or other Indians have such feelings has been denied; but I, who have lived and hunted with them, know that all men have souls alike—mayhap some deeper-buried than others beneath the crust of time and circumstance, yet all there for the finding.

Ruth and I ate our evening meal together, while Grim crunched a bone contentedly at our sides. Both of us, as our garments had given out, had replaced them with others of very soft skin, while in this cold winter weather we wore furs as, did the Crees. When the meal was done we covered over the little fire in the center of the lodge, and stepped to the door.

Five minutes later we were in the lodge of council—a large structure, half skin and half brush. Around the fire were ranged the old men of the village, and the chiefs; and after a dignified silence the calumet was passed around from hand to hand, among the very old men only, for with these people tobacco was rather in the nature of a burnt-offering, and was never smoked for the pleasure therein. Another silence, then the oldest chief arose and very briefly directed Ruth to speak to them as she wished.

CHAPTER XII

THE MOOSE OF MYSTERY

I WOULD THAT I might give here the speech that Ruth made to those Crees, there by the dim light of the little fire, her yellow hair flashing forth from the wolf-fur hood in long tendrils, her eyes striving to pierce through the darkness to those stolid faces about her. She did not speak their language at all well, and I saw plainly that the hearing had been given her out of courtesy alone. They were our friends, were these Crees, because we were the friends of Radisson, and they would do all for us that friends might.

At length she finished and turned away. I stepped forward when the old chief had gravely risen and thanked her, and led her to the entrance. When I returned, the same old man rose and addressed me.

"Our brother Brave Eyes has heard the words of the Yellow Lily. They were like the dew upon the trees at dawn—sparkling and refreshing, but not fit to quench the thirst of the warriors. There is much that we do not understand, and we hope that Brave Eyes will set our minds at rest."

I waited a space, knowing that this would add dignity to my words. Even as I rose to my feet, a noise of dogs came from without, the flap of the door was pushed aside and The Keeper. The Arrow and Radisson entered and flitted to their seats in the Council. This seemed like a good omen to me, and I took heart again.

Now I appealed to the warriors direct, strove to wake them to consciousness of what my message meant, applied all that I said to their life and daily acts. As I went on, the words flowed almost of themselves, and I, who had ever been a clumsy, gawky lout, felt with a thrill that I was commanding these men. Yet it was not I, as none knew better. It was a Something that spoke in and through me, until in the end I felt a great fear of what that Something might be. None the less, I said what I had to say, and so seated myself again, the sweat standing out on my brow.

For a long, long time there was no sound within the lodge. Then I saw The Keeper rise to his feet and walk out beside the fire, standing a moment like a dark statue.

"My brothers," he said in Cree, "we have listened to very great words. In my own land the Great Spirit has sent his Blackrobes to speak such words to us, and we have listened. I am very old, my brothers. These words are sweet in my ears. But my white brothers, Brave Eyes and White Eagle, have not heard all. The Great Spirit has not whispered to them of the Mighty One. Perhaps he has sent them that the Mighty One should be slain, and that the Cree nation should know which was the True Great Spirit. I have ended."

I did not understand the conclusion of this speech, but I did understand the half-audible gasp of horror that ran through the lodge. It brought back to me the time when I was a little fellow, and had gone to meeting one day with my father and mother. While the preacher was thundering forth, I had escaped from mother and toddled away to look up in laughing wonder at the tall figure of Alec Gordon, with his stiff starched bands. In that moment the same shuddering gasp had echoed through the folk, and I heard later that no few of them had looked to see me fall stricken.

So around the Council lodge ran the same whisper and was gone instantly. I wondered what sacrilege The Keeper had uttered, and stared at Uchichak as he gravely rose, took up the calumet, lit it, and waved it to the four corners of the heavens. Then he replaced it and turned toward me.

"My brother Ta-cha-noon-tia is our friend. His words are the words of a friend. He is a great warrior and an old man, and his Great Spirit is very strong. But it is not our Great Spirit who whispers in his ear, and we are afraid. I will tell my brothers of our Great Spirit."

With a single stride he went to the door and flung open the flap dramatically. Before us in the sky flamed the northern lights—grotesque sheeted figures of lambent flame, dancing here and yon, rising, falling, many-colored.

"The Spirits of the Dead who Dance," he affirmed, in a single Cree word. "My brothers the Great Spirit of our fathers is mighty. This is his sign to his children. When we have passed the last trail, we too shall join our fathers in the Spirit-dance across the heavens. This is the sign that our Great Spirit has given us. And now I shall tell you of the Mystery."

I would have sprung up and made ready answer, but a hand gripped my arm and I found Radisson behind me. I remembered that Indian ways were not our ways, and that when Uchichak had finished I could speak, and not until then.

"My brothers, our Great Spirit, from the days of our fathers, has sent us a messenger. Sometimes it is a man, sometimes it is an animal." His voice lowered almost to a whisper, and the hush was intense. "My brothers, it is more than an animal, more than a little brother of the forest, who are chiefs, we of the Council, know that this messenger is none other than the Great Spirit himself, who comes to watch over his children."

For an instant there was dead silence, Uchichak standing with bowed head. Only the sound of heavy breathing filled the lodge until he continued more firmly.

"My brothers, when I was very young the messenger was a White Beaver, larger and more cunning than ever beaver was before him. When I was a young man the Mighty One had vanished, and in his place was another Mighty One. How did we know this? I will tell you.

"One of our young men brought the news that in the Barren Places was a mighty moose, larger than any moose ever seen. He had followed the tracks, and had come to a bear, slain by the moose. There were three young men in the village who said they would hunt this moose. Our old men warned them, saying that the young man had been led to the bear in token that the moose wished us well. Perhaps he was a Mighty One. But the young men refused to listen and went forth with their dogs.

"My brothers, you have heard the tale of Spotted Lynx, Two Horns and Yellow Cloud. They hunted for many weeks. The Mighty One did not wish to harm them. But at last they found him feeding, and wounded him. My brothers, are any of those young men among you? Have you seen their faces in the lodges of their people? Have they returned to their fathers?"

A single half-suppressed groan broke from one of the old men. There was no doubt that the tale was true. I reflected that if three hunters, armed with bow and spear, had gone out against that terrible moose, there might well have been small chance of their returning safe. But The Crane did not pause long.

"We have heard how the hunters of the Chippewa nation have sought him, and have fled home like women to their people. Our fathers have told us how, when they were little children, the Great Spirit had whispered to them that the Crees should not seek to hunt the Mighty One, and should not seek to hunt in the hills of the Barren Places. It is in these hills that the Mighty One now dwells, and the Chippewas fear them also.

"Sometimes the Mighty One travels far. My brothers, you have heard how Brave Eyes met him. You have seen that he favored Brave Eyes and did not kill him, but sent him to be our brother. The heart of Brave Eyes is very strong. We know that it holds no fear. Now that he knows who the Mighty One is whose horns he felt, now that he knows it was our Great Spirit himself, Brave Eyes will not fear to say that he was wrong."

Uchichak drew his furs about him and resumed his seat. The eyes of the Council, one by one, were slowly turned on me. But not until I felt Radisson's hand relax on my arm did I rise to speak.

"My brothers," I said with some difficulty, "I speak in a strange tongue. I can find no words in it to say that I did not speak to you rightly before. The Crane has told me that the Spirits of the Dead who Dance are signs from your Great Spirit. How is it, then, that the same signs have come to me and my brother the White Eagle and to my sister the Yellow Lily, very far from here? How is it that this sign comes to my white brothers also?"

There was a little stir at this, and I heard the Keeper grunt in appreciation.

"Listen, my brothers. I have told you of the sign in the water, which the Great Spirit has sent to his white children, through his own Son. I wish you to remember this, and it may be that you will accept this sign. As to your Mighty One, he is not a Messenger sent by the Great Spirit; he is a messenger of the Evil Spirit."

I had looked for another stir at these words, but none came. Instead, there was silence—the silence of apprehension, of waiting.

"My brothers, you do not like my words, but your hearts are open. Your ears are not closed to the whisper of the Great Spirit, and you will listen. If the Mighty One was your friend and protector, would he have slain your young men? Would he not have sent them home as he has sent the other hunters, like foolish women?"

I paused again, taking full advantage of this favorite trick of Indian Oratory.

"Listen, my brothers. My Great Spirit whispers to me. He says that your Mighty One is false. He says that there is only one Great Spirit, and that He wishes you to accept the sign in the water. He says that it is for this purpose He brought me to you. He asks you whether you will accept this sign that you believe in Him."

With this rather abrupt close I sat down. There was a long silence as they turned over my words carefully, slowly, weighing each one. Finally the old wizened head-chief, whose single eagle-feather gleamed oddly in the red light, answered me.

"My brother, you have spoken well. Your words have satisfied the thirst of the warriors, as the spring that bubbles in the forest. Yet we were afraid at them, for we feared that our Great Spirit would be angry.

"You have said that the sign of the Spirits of the Dead has been sent to you also. That is well. The Great Spirit has whispered to me. He whispered in my ear that you, my brother, and my brother Eagle also, should prove to us that the Mighty One is a messenger of the Evil Spirit. You have told us how your Great Spirit sent His Son to you, and how you killed Him. We would not have treated Him thus, my brother. Our ears are open. We would have feasted Him with venison and listened to Him.

"The Great Spirit has whispered to me that you should seek the Mighty One. We know that there is no fear in your heart, and that the White Eagle is very wise and good. Perhaps the Great Spirit will help you. If you slay the Mighty One we will know that we have been wrong, and that our fathers have been wrong, and we will accept the sign in the water."

Weak and shaking, the old man sat down and covered his face. One by one the chiefs stood up and spoke in the same vein. One by one they agreed that if Radisson and I should slay the Moose, they would accept the "sign in the water," for thus only could I represent the symbol of baptism to them. Uchichak made a splendid speech, and I was right glad to find here in the wilderness men whose minds were so open, so free to conviction. Their beliefs were simple and earnest, and while there was small hope that they would or could accept the gospel of peace, merely to bring them to a knowledge of the True God would be a tremendous conquest.

So the Council ended. Radisson accompanied me to the lodge of Ruth, where we told her all that had taken place, and of the gage of battle which had been flung before us. That it would be accepted by Radisson I had no doubt.

"Aye, lad," he said in answer to my eager question, "I may hold to no faith over-much, but in this matter I am with you—if only for the sake of little Ruth here."

"Not that!" she flashed out at him quickly. "Pray, Uncle Pierre, have you no deeper thought than this? Look deep down in your heart, and say no if you dare!"

Radisson looked down at her, then at me, and in his weary eyes I saw what I had but seldom found in his face. In that moment I knew that even from us he had kept his real self hidden.

"Yes, child," he replied softly. "I hesitated to acknowledge it, but it is true. I may not be of your faith, but I will do this thing for the sake of Him who suffered for us all, and in the trust that through us these poor, faithful friends of ours may be given a light to lighten their darkness."

Wherewith he rose and left us suddenly, nor did he ever allude to that conversation again, until the day he left us. But Ruth and I sat silent for a little space, wondering.

"It is a fearsome thing," I murmured at last, "how this superstition has laid hold on such men as Uchichak. Why, the Mighty One is no more than a beast—cunning, merciless, but still a beast. With such men as Radisson and the Mohawks with me, what is there to fear?"

"Softly, Davie," smiled Ruth a little sadly. "It is not so easy as may seem to you. Did ever an easy thing accomplish aught in the world? It is the things we fight for and suffer for that are worth while, that bring the Word to the world. It was never God's way to make the path easy for those who bear His Word."

I wondered at her not a little. There was a light in her sweet face that I had never seen before, and something in her manner smote me to the heart, so that I bade her good-night and left her to sleep.

And ever since that night I have thought that Ruth spoke not of herself, for her words were fraught with prophecy.

For the next few days the four of us were very busy. We decided that if the work must be done it should be done at once, and we made ready without delay. I think Radisson, despite his words of that night, was eager to be off and away into the westing lands where no man had been, for it was ever his wont to seek beyond the known things.

The Crees were ready enough to help us with all that we asked. Uchichak it was who gave us his dogs and sled, whereon we loaded food and our fusils, with what store of powder and ball we had. It was settled that after the next heavy fall of snow we should set forth, and by the signs of the country the Crees declared that a storm was not far off.

Indeed, it came within the week—two days of heavy, drifting snow and high wind. And when it came we knew that ere long we would be parted from our little lass. But the manner of that parting, and the ending of it, was in no wise what we had looked forward to.

CHAPTER XIII

THE RAIDERS

NOW IT may be that the things I have to relate will seem strange and un-Christian and wondrous, even as they do to me. Yet are they but the truth. In that far Northern land many such things come to pass, for there man is very close to the forces of the world, and whether it be that his mind is quickened by the dread silence of the snows, or whether there is in truth a nearness to God in that silence. I know not. It has often vexed me and the answer is not yet.

But this much I do know. Holding to none of the superstitions around me, I then believed and do still affirm that the whole matter of the Moose of Mystery, the Mighty One, was under the direction of some Higher Power, and that Gib o' Clarclach came to his triumph and his end through that same guidance. Howbeit, I had best leave you to judge for yourselves.

That storm came upon us and closed us in our lodges for two days. On the third morning it was decided that we should start forth just as soon as the crust had formed strong enough to bear dogs and sled. In the meantime, Uchichak and I went forth upon a last hunt, thinking to bring in a caribou or elk, for with the winter the bison had drifted far to the south of us.

Two days of idleness and gorging, as was the custom of the Crees, had well-nigh finished the stock of food in the village. Therefore most of the men fared forth on the hunt. Radisson and the two Mohawks trailed together, admitting none other to their company, and on the second morning thereafter we four were to set out upon our quest. According to custom, the warriors set out in small groups or singly, scattering in all directions. Ruth was engaged in making deerskin scabbards for the fusils, since in that terrific cold it was impossible to set fingers to iron.

Uchichak and I were accompanied by a lively young brave named Wapistan, or The Marten, who had often gone out with us, and whose tracking powers were remarkable. As ever, we were armed only with bows and flint-tipped arrows. My own weapon, which I had made with great care, was a source of great interest to the Crees, for it was full twice as long and thick as theirs, and even Uchichak could scarcely bend it, although to me the trick came easily enough. I would never be as expert as was The Crane, but when it came to distance I could overshoot him greatly. This, however, was more by reason of my greater strength, for which quality of body I later thanked God most heartily.

The fierceness of the storm seemed to have driven most of the larger animals to the shelter of the hills, and although we circled widely to the east of the village and then to the north, by that evening we had found nothing save a few rabbits, which barely were sufficient for our own needs. As there was another day ahead of us, we camped that night beneath some willows on the bank of an ice-clad river. I urged Uchichak to push forward to the hills in the northeast, but he refused stoutly.

"Those are the Ghost Hills, brother. There walks the Mighty One, and the Spirits of the Dead who Dance. We can hear them singing in the wind. We must not disturb them."

All that evening The Crane was very silent and downcast, and I came to know that he considered that this was our last trip together. To his mind, the Great Spirit would never allow me to come back from that hunt against the Mighty One. The Ghost Hills were sacred, and were about to be impiously profaned. Indeed, since that meeting of the Council we had come in for no small share of reverence from all the warriors, who held that we were bravely going to our deaths. I learned later

that it had been decided that the Yellow Lily should become
the adopted daughter of the tribe, should we fail to return.

Early in the morning the three of us left our brush shelter
and started forth, determined to avoid the disgrace of returning
to the village empty-handed. Now we circled back toward the
south again, overlooking no patch of woods where elk or deer
might be sheltering. The morning was still young when we came
to a break of heavy-laden pines, and started through them
warily. Suddenly a cry from Wapistan, at one side, called us to
him.

"Come quickly!"

We found him standing in the midst of some bushes, where
the snow had been kicked away in a wide circle, affording access
to the tender green shoots beneath. But there was no expression
of joy on his face, and as we came up The Crane halted abruptly.

"Let us go away quickly," he muttered. I was amazed at this,
for it was plain to me that here was the bed of a moose, and I
stared at the two men until Wapistan led me over to the side
of the little clearing.

"Let my brother look upon the tracks of the Mighty One,"
was all he said. There before me were such tracks as I had never
seen—great imprints of sharp hoofs that could only have been
made by the giant moose which had attacked us in the beginning. I have hunted many moose, since then, but never have I
found such a trail as that.

"Listen, Uchichak," I said, trembling with eagerness. "If he
is the Mighty One, he must have been sent to us, for we are far
from the Hills. Let us follow. I will hunt him, you need not."

"The Mighty One walks on the storm," murmured The Crane,
glancing around apprehensively. None the less, my words had
impressed him. "We will see whither the tracks lead. It may be
that the Great Spirit has sent him to his children. He may lead
us to a herd of elk. We will follow a little way."

And therein was the beginning of our strange pilgrimage.

Without delay we started out, Wapistan leading and Uchichak bringing up the rear. The great caution displayed by these hunters told me more than any words could have done that our quest was a dangerous one. With bows strung and ready, every aisle of the forest was searched ahead of us, and with every crack of sticks and trees in the great frost I could see Wapistan spring to alertness. But all around us was nothing save the deathly silence, through which the frost-crackles and the "sluff-sluff" of our snowshoes sounded loud.

Mile after mile we plowed along, from patch to patch of forest, and still the deep tracks of the giant beast led us onward. The fresh-fallen snow had made heavy going for him, since at each step he plunged through to his knees. The Crees might consider that he walked on the wind, but for my own part I thought him a feckless creature to leave the shelter of the Hills in such a storm. And in that thought I neglected the workings of Providence, as I later admitted readily enough.

The trail presently led us to a fairly large river, and out across the ice. The other bank was bordered with thick trees, and as we neared them I turned to The Crane and smiled.

"If the Mighty One walked on the storm, Uchichak, it looks as though men had also been able to walk there."

But the Indians had already caught sight of the dark trail on the farther shore, and with a guttural exclamation of surprise we all dashed forward. There in the shelter of the trees the snow was not so deep, and the tracks of the Mighty One led us straight to a deep trail plowed in the snow, where they were lost.

"Are they other hunters from the village?" I asked in my ignorance. The two Crees kicked away their snowshoes and crept about examining the trail, while I leaned on my bow. It was plain enough that the Moose had gone forward in this path, where the snow had been worn away and packed deep for him, whereat I began to think better of his sense.

Uchichak straightened up suddenly, and at sight of his face I knew that something was wrong—terribly wrong. His usual stolidity had given place to rage and grief, and he turned to me with a flame in his dark eyes.

"My brother, we must hasten to the village at once. Men have come and gone, and they are not of our own people."

Still I realized nothing of what he meant, although his face sobered me.

"Then do you go," I returned, "while I continue on the trail of the Mighty One—" But Wapistan had sprung to my side, eager and wrathful.

"Brave Eyes cannot read the trail," he cried sharply. "See, here have gone many men—two or three tens of men. Their tracks lead away from the village, and with them goes a dog-sled. They travel toward the Ghost Hills, and their snowshoes are of Chippewa make. Let us hasten, my brothers!"

Then I groaned, for I remembered what Radisson had said of Gib, called The Pike, and his Chippewa followers. If these men had come to the village when the hunters were away, what had happened?

Right speedily was all thought of the Mighty One forgotten, as we took up the trail in desperate haste toward the village. Wapistan went on to say that it was very fresh, that the band had not passed us more than an hour previously, and in no long time his words were borne out. For, as we turned a sharp bend in the river-trail, we came upon two men striding rapidly toward us. They were not more than a hundred yards away, and I did not need Uchichak's hasty exclamation to tell me that they were Chippewas. For one was our old friend Soan-ge-ta-ha, though the other I knew not.

For a bare second we stared at each other, then I saw the Chippewa chief throw off the coverings of a musket. I dashed my two companions headlong, just as the weapon roared out and gave vent to a cloud of smoke. The bullet sang overhead, and at this unprovoked and cowardly attack I picked up my strung bow and drew it taut.

The two Chippewas had darted aside just after the chief fired, and were speeding for the shelter of the trees. But my arrow sped faster than they. Even as Uchichak and Wapistan darted forward, I saw Brave Heart stumble, and the musket flew far from him. He was up and running again, however, but the brief pause had given my vengeful friends a lead. All four disappeared among the trees, with wild cries that thrilled my heart.

I followed slowly after them, glad that my savage aim had not gone true, for in all my life I had never shed the heart-blood of a man. That these Chippewas were enemies there was no doubt, and I prudently stopped to recover the musket dropped by the chief, for such things were valuable. A brief wonder came to me that the weapon had not dismayed the two Crees, but I hastened to follow them in among the trees. As I did so, I caught a glimpse of something dark speeding toward us from the direction of the village, but I stopped not to see what it was.

From the trees and bushes came the sound of men struggling, and when I had broken through I saw the four in front. Wapistan was calmly sitting in the snow, wiping his long flint knife, and I turned from him with a shudder. Soan-ge-ta-ha and Uchichak were at handgrips, but The Crane plainly had the mastery over the Chippewa chief, in whose shoulder still stood my arrow. Even as I plunged forward through the snow, Brave Heart bent backward, the knife dropped from his nerveless fingers, and Uchichak stood up to meet me.

"It was a good fight, brother!" he said calmly. "This Chippewa dog is only faint from loss of blood. The Marten has sharp teeth, and is a warrior. Good!"

I kneeled over Brave Heart, pulled the arrow through his shoulder-muscles, and roughly bound up the already freezing wound. As I did so, I told the others of the dark object that I had seen approaching, and Wapistan slipped away. The Crane aided me in getting Brave Heart up with his back against a stump, and barely had we done so when there was a crash of bushes behind us, and in swept Radisson, The Keeper, and Swift Arrow, leading the same dog-sled which had been prepared for our hunt of the Mighty One. The Chippewa chief opened his eyes.

"Soan-ge-ta-ha," burst out Radisson angrily in English, "your heart is bad! You have led your warriors against the Crees, stealing upon them in the night, and you shall suffer for it bitterly!"

"What has happened?" I cried out, a great fear rising in me. "What does it all mean?"

Brave Heart smiled cruelly, the two Mohawks stood impassive. Radisson turned to me with a sudden sob shaking his great frame, and his white-bearded face seemed shot with lightnings as he made reply in Cree, that the warriors might understand.

"What does it mean? It means that The Pike is on his last war-path, Davie! Last night a band of thirty Chippewas burst on the village. The few men held them back until most of the women could escape with some few things, then—then the village was destroyed."

A grunt broke from Uchichak, and his hand went to his knife as he stood over the wounded chief. But I flung him away, a question hot on my lips.

"Was it Ruth they were after? Did they harm her?"

"Yes and no, lad. They bore her away captive on a sled. Fortunately, these dogs and our sled had been hidden out of their reach. When the Mohawks and I returned we took them and came after. You shall go forward with us, and we will follow the party."

"What can we do against them?" I exclaimed hopelessly.

"We can watch and wait," returned Radisson grimly, with a significant look at the two gaunt warriors beside him. "Uchichak, do you take this Chippewa back and hold him captive. Gather your hunters speedily—even now they are coming in. Send a runner to the village of Talking Owl and bid his young men join you. Then follow our trail, even though it may lead to the Ghost Hills. There, perhaps, The Pike will imagine that you do not dare follow."

Uchichak said nothing. He and Wapistan jerked Brave Heart to his feet, replaced his snowshoes for him, and the three departed. So suddenly and unexpectedly had the dire news broken upon me, that I stood as if dazed. Radisson came and put a kindly hand on my shoulder.

"Come, lad, all is not lost. They will not harm the little maid, and we must hasten on their trail. Not even The Pike would dare harm her while their chief is a captive. Come, there is work for us ahead. Now tell me your tale as we go forward."

Brokenly, I told him how we had come upon the trail. When I finished, Radisson's face was lit with a stern glow, and he raised a hand to the Mohawks.

"My brothers, the Great Spirit is fighting for us! The Mighty One has led Brave Eyes to the trail. He will lead us on where the trail is lost!"

And that was the manner in which the madness of Radisson began—a madness, I think, which was sent by the Great Spirit of whom he spoke.

CHAPTER XIV

THE PURSUIT

WHEN I speak of madness, I mean nothing else. From that moment the old man was daft, as it seemed to me. We two led the way, the Mohawks following after the sled, and Radisson set such a place as I never traveled before or since.

The mighty energy of the old man dominated us all. From his words I soon saw that he had become filled with the idea that the Moose had been sent to lead us to Ruth again, until presently the uncanny thought of it laid hold on me likewise. We took up the trail of the raiders, which after a few miles crossed the river and struck off straight for the northeast, with the moose-tracks still following it.

Mile after mile we swung behind us. I wondered at Radisson's words—"where the trail is lost"—for it seemed that a child could follow such a plain, deep track as this. But he had not lived his life in the wilderness for naught. As we went forward, he told of how the raiders must have left before the great storm, and have traveled through it, to spring on the village with Indian cunning when they knew the hunters would be gone.

Their object was plain enough, for Gib thought to get a firm hold on Radisson by the capture of Ruth, and perhaps to sell that advantage to the English or French. Both nations had wronged the terrible old man deeply, and both would be like to go wild when they heard that he was loose in his own land again. In the old days the mere magic of his name, the terror inspired by his countless daring escapades and adventures, had more than once swept the Bay clear of his foes. I have often thought that had the French not betrayed him so shamefully, and had the English not misused his great powers so basely, one nation or the other would ere now have ruled all the land from the Colonies to the Bay. There are wars and rumors of wars in the land, however, and I have even lately heard a wild rumor that our armies have conquered all the Canadas; though this is hardly possible, to my mind. But to return to my tale.

There was some dried meat on the sledge, and this we ate as we traveled, without stop. The Chippewa party, fearful of pursuit, were putting on all speed in a desperate effort to gain the shelter of the Hills before they were overtaken. The trail was fresh, and they could not go faster than did we, for they were handicapped by the sled which bore Ruth.

From Radisson I learned that Gib had cunningly prevented his raiders from injuring the people of the village. He no doubt knew that if Ruth alone were carried off, the Crees would hesitate long before venturing to follow him into the sacred Hills. But the savage instincts of his followers had upset his crafty plans. Soan-ge-ta-ha and another had stolen back to pillage and burn and slay, thinking to catch up easily with the party. But for us they would have done so, and now not even the Ghost Hills would stay the vengeful Crees from the pursuit.

At evening we halted for a brief half-hour, to bait and rest the dogs. Now the weeks of hardening and hunting began to bear fruit, for I had stood that terrific pace nearly as well as the rest. My ribs were still somewhat sore at times, but in the main I was heartier and stronger than ever in my life before.

The rest was grateful to us all, and at this time we loaded the fusils, together with the musket taken from Brave Heart, and covered them carefully on the sled. We might have need of them at any time, and to load was no short work. For some time I had seen no signs of Ruth's sled in the trail we followed, and spoke of it to the Keeper.

"It is there," he grunted. "They are following it, hiding it beneath their tracks."

"That looks as if they were getting ready to lose the trail," put in Radisson. He seemed to give no thought to this possibility, taking it as a matter of course, and the Mohawks only nodded. It seemed strange to me, but I held my peace.

When the Spirit of the Dead began to dance in the sky we took up the march again, goading the weary dogs to the trail. Faint rumbles as of thunder seemed to come from the heavens, but ever we slapped on and on across the snows, while grotesque shadows fell all around us as the lights quivered above in lambent blue and purple flames. It was a wondrous spectacle, far beyond any that I had seen at home, where the lights were a common occurrence, and I gave the Crees small blame for naming them as they did. To an ignorant people those flaring fires of God must indeed have seemed like spirits leaping over the skies.

The deep trail led us straight through forest and wild, open levels of snow. Once we came to a camping-place of the Chippewas, where they too had made a brief halt for food and rest. Far beyond lay the deep forest, and a wide curving line of taller trees tokened that there was some large river before us, or mayhap a lake.

And a lake it proved to be, set in the midst of trees, with a small stream flowing from it. All was ice-coated, swept bare of snow by the wind, and the trail led straight to this sheet of ice. Radisson laughed grimly when we found this.

"Hold up, Davie. We must have a council here. Do you stop with the dogs?"

I obeyed, while the others set off in different directions across the ice. They returned quickly enough, and with their first words I knew that the trail was lost.

"They have scattered on the ice," spoke up Swift Arrow. "Three parties have gone away from the farther shore."

Radisson nodded, his deep eyes searching the trees around us.

"Then how do we know which to follow?" I cried in dismay. "Which party took the sled with them?"

"That we know not lad," he made answer as if to a child. "They have followed after the sled, hiding its track. It might be with any of the three parties. They will swing out in a wide circle and then straight for the hills. No matter which we follow, we lose time. An excellent trick to fool children with, chief."

The Keeper merely grunted, while I stared at them aghast. Why did Radisson take this so calmly? But he gave me no time to question.

"Did you find it?" he asked the Mohawks simply. Swift Arrow made answer.

"The Mighty One's trail goes alone. It goes toward the east, where lies the shadow of the Ghost Hills."

Then in a flash I saw it all. Radisson proposed to abandon the Chippewa trails and follow that of the beast! The belief that the animal had been sent to guide us had overpowered all his woodcraft and subtlety, and I flung out at him in wild protest.

"It is madness!" I concluded angrily. "Better to lose time and still be on the track of the enemy, than to follow a wandering beast!"

"Rail not against the wisdom of old men," exclaimed Radisson sternly, his voice ringing with confidence. "The Mighty One is guiding us, Davie. Do you lead, Keeper, while we come after. We must break trail now, and it will be no light labor."

Raging against the old man's madness, for so I deemed it, I set out with The Keeper to break trail. The Moose plunged straight ahead for the Hills, and his long legs had sunk almost to the shoulder at every step. I wondered how far ahead of us he might be, and when The Keeper knelt down quickly to smell the trail I knew that we must be close upon him.

The fortitude and strength that dwelt in the frame of the old chief was marvellous. We broke the trail by turns, our shoes stamping deep down through the soft crust at each step, until it required every ounce of endurance we possessed to keep on with the labor. Miles of it, hours of it, passed by, and still we kept on at the same terrific pace. At times Radisson and Swift Arrow relieved us, but ever we headed straight for the Ghost Hills, whose tree-clad and rocky summits now rose clear against the lambent sky. As we went, I began to fall into Radisson's way of thinking. Perhaps, after all, that uncanny Moose was leading us, guiding us straight to our goal. And whether it were the silence of these waste and desolate barrens around, or some inner feeling of the night, I gained confidence that He who in truth led us would not let harm come to the little maid.

It seemed hours before we rested again, and this time I flung myself down on a skin from the sled, huddling among the dogs for warmth, and slept. Those three old men must have been made of iron, for when I awakened I saw The Keeper sitting just as I had left him, alert and keen-eyed as ever, while Swift Arrow and Radisson were talking in low tones.

The poor brutes that hauled the sled suffered even more than we did. They were worn to death, and before we started out again, having fed them what we dared from our slender stock of food, we cut up our single robe which had covered the guns, and bound their bleeding feet as best we might. They fell to the trail limping, but there must have been something of the Indian stolidity in them, for all that long march I heard no cry, no whimper, burst from their throats.

Now, for the first time, I thought of Grim. What had happened to him? Where was he? At my questions Radisson smiled.

"He is faithful still, lad. They said in the village that he defended Ruth until Gib would have killed him, when the lass consented to go with them to save his life. Grim stayed ever at her side, and is like enough with her now."

This cheered me mightily, small hope though it were. Well I knew the wiliness of that old sheep-dog, and that while Ruth was endangered he would watch over her even as my father would have done. When I took up the weary labor again it was with better heart and more confident spirit than since the start.

Now we knew that we could not be far from the end of the terrible journey. Or at least my three comrades knew it, for I refused to admit that there was aught save madness in keeping to the moose-track. The snatch of sleep and food had cleared my mind from the influence of the night, and as we slapped on over the snows I railed bitterly at myself for ever having consented to it.

Slowly the hills ahead, purple in the unearthly, flitting lights, drew closer and towered ahead of us. Slowly the wide expanse of snow broke into little rises, then we found ourselves among the first of the Ghost Hills. Before long I knew why they had received that name.

They seemed to break straight out of the ground—great masses of black rock like that on the coast below Rathesby, at home. As we drew among them, still following that gigantic track left plain for us to read, I saw that despite the heavy snow the black masses of rock stood out bare and bleak, closing around us and shutting out the lights above.

The trail led downward now—down in a winding line among the towering crags, and we were passing over still deeper snow, which had drifted from the hills. As we wound through the dark passages a swift, chill wind smote us and cut to the marrow. It was not my first taste of the bitter wind of the Northland, which is infinitely harder to endure than the most silent cold, however great it may be.

Thus we were literally swallowed up in that terrible abyss of rock and snow, and the weird feeling of the place affected even our dogs, who growled and shivered. All was dead silent, except for the rush and howl of the wind, which seemed to shoot down through those narrow pits of darkness, until we could with difficulty stand against it. From somewhere ahead droned out the long, eerie howl of a wolf, drifting to us on the wind. I saw

Swift Arrow, ahead of me, pause and throw up his head; then into the teeth of the gale he cast an answering howl—one as perfect as the other, which drew a sharp yelp from the dogs. By this time I comprehended how on board the "Lass" Radisson had so amazed and shamed us all, and had even learned a little of the mimicry myself.

It fearful to drive ahead through that gale, which sent the icy particles of snow against us like tiny knives, and to know that outside and above, the night was silent and windless. Indeed, there was never any rest within the Ghost Hills, and I could well realize why the Indians dreaded and avoided them.

By now I was more than ever sure that we were not only on the wrong track, but that this Mighty One was sent by the foul fiend to lead us astray and into danger of the worst. The passage of those hills was terrible to the body and to the soul. As we drew deeper into the darkness, weird echoes were set flying by our shoes and the wind and the voices of us. These were not borne past, but seemed to eddy up overhead, as though some flux of the wind caught and whirled them back toward us.

The Keeper had been in the lead, Radisson following. Of a sudden, as we came to a space somewhat lighter, I saw that the chief had vanished! I uttered a single cry that rebounded about in mad echoes, but Swift Arrow gripped me as I turned in terror.

"Peace! Ta-cha-noon-tia has but gone ahead to see what lies before."

With the calm words my fear passed, and I was ashamed. After all, we were in the hand of God, and if He willed that evil should come to us, then it would come. So I quelled my terror and pressed on after the sledge. A moment more, and the passage was done with.

Turning the corner of a sharp cliff, we found ourselves out in the night again, standing on a ridge of bare black rock. At our side stood The Keeper. Behind towered those terrible cliffs, but ahead was a little forested basin, alight with the fires of the sky and stretching ahead to hills in the distance. Radisson turned to the Mohawk with a question.

"My father, the tracks of the Mighty One are lost and I do not see them. But below us are the lodges of warriors."

I looked again at the stretch of wooded country. Sure enough, I could see black groups of something that might well be huts or lodges, but there was no sign of fire to cheer us.

"The Mighty One has led us well," shouted Radisson triumphantly. "We have arrived before them we seek! Let us rest, brothers, and make merry, for we are masters of the stronghold of The Pike, and his fate is in our hands!"

So for the rest of that night we lay in the snow behind the ledge, while over us the wind howled down into the cleft of rocks, and around us the poor weary dogs huddled in shivering groups, for we dared light no fire, and had like to have frozen in the great cold. But the Moose had led us aright, and the madness of Radisson was justified—in part.

CHAPTER XV

OUTGENERALED

IT WAS not far from dawn when we arrived at the ridge,
or ledge that ran along the cliffs, with an easy descent over
the rolling snows to the basin beneath. But as the dancing dead
men paled in the skies, the cold became too bitter for any of
us. It was necessary that we light a fire to keep from perishing,
and the two Mohawks disappeared to right and left. It was so
cold that sleep was impossible, weary as we were.

However, The Keeper returned and motioned to us that we
should accompany him, and in a few moments we were gathered
in a deep cleft amid the rocks, to one side of the terrible passage
by which we had come. Here The Arrow met us with some dry
wood and birch-bark, and before long we were gathered about
a smokeless fire, which at least served to permit of our sleeping.

With one of us on watch at a time, the day passed away. After
noon, I was wakened and placed on guard at the crest of the
ridge, overlooking the basin. A little later, I saw a number of
moving objects off to the west, and speedily wakened my companions, with a great relief and joy in my heart. The Mighty
One had led us aright! Doubtless he himself had for years made
his home in these hills where he was safe from man, and by
following his trail we had chanced on a short cut to the heart
of the Ghost Hills, while the Chippewa band had been forced
to take a longer trail.

The moving objects resolved themselves into the forms of
men as they drew nearer, clear and distinct in that atmosphere

which seemed to bring all things close to us. We watched silently, each knowing that the others perceived all, and could
make out a sled with some dark object on it. There were barely
a dozen men in the party, so we knew the others had taken a
longer detour in order to throw off and delay pursuit, and would
doubtless arrive later.

"What will we do?" I murmured to Radisson. "We have little
food, yet we cannot make an attack on them."

He turned to the Mohawks, and the three old men spoke
for a few moments in the Iroquois tongue. Meanwhile, the
Chippewa party had come nigh the huts, and presently I could
see the light flare of fire-smoke rising from the midst. At the
distance, it was impossible to make out form or feature, yet I
had no doubt that the burden lifted from the sled, and the dark
dot beside it, were Ruth and the faithful Grim.

"It is hard to tell," said Radisson in French, his fine face
wrinkled in perplexity. "We cannot make an open attack, for
that fiend Larue would kill the little maid sooner than give her
up. It is plain that they fear no enemy, since they are in the open
and that smoke could be seen afar.

"There are a score of them still out, and it must be that they
do not fear Uchichak's men. Possibly they have come along a
trail that Swift Arrow discovered and followed last year. He
says it could be defended by a few against an army. I see naught
to do save to wait until night, and try to steal down and get the
little maid. Could we but get her up here, we might defend that
pass behind us against a thousand."

Swift Arrow grunted approval. "The Crees cannot break
through the western trail," he said. "They grow faint at the sight
of blood. The Chippewas are women, also. To-night we will
steal down and take away Yellow Lily."

I thought over his words, as I gazed on the encampment
below. If he was right, we might expect no aid, for that terrible
gulf through which we had come was unknown to all men, and

the trail followed by Gib was doubtless secured against the Crees. But if only Uchichak—

"Listen!" I cried out with the thought blazing in me. "We are but four, and three of us could hold the mouth of that gully—even this whole crest. I cannot drive dogs, nor do I know the ways of the trail well enough; but Swift Arrow or The Keeper could take the sled and drive back, bringing Uchichak and his men by the trail of the Mighty One. Then to-night you and the remaining Mohawks can attempt the rescue of Ruth."

Radisson considered the matter in silence, glanced at the impassive chiefs, and received a grunt which tokened approval. With no more parley, Great Swift Arrow drew down his fur hood and picked up the thong which served as a dog-whip.

"I will go," he declared calmly as ever. "I will find you waiting in the pass?"

"In the pass," echoed Radisson.

Without more ado, the dogs, snarling and protesting, were forced into the harness, The Arrow cracked his whip, and he was gone along the ridge toward the mouth of the pass, as if the long trip before him was no more than a pleasure excursion. He had left the guns, all save one, together with most of the dried meat.

Radisson and I went forth to a group of pines which grew in the shelter of the ridge, and when we returned with some store of dry wood we found The Keeper curled up asleep. The Indians seemed to have the power of sleep whenever they wished, and Radisson chuckled.

"Do you keep guard, lad, while I sleep also. Wake me at midday."

I nodded, for I felt no great need of sleep, and the old man sat down beside his friend, feet to the fire. I left the cranny in the rocks and went forth a few paces into the sunlight's warmth, where I could overlook the encampment of The Pike. Here, crouched down in hiding, I set myself to wait as patiently as might be until the appointed time should pass.

The camp below was too far away for any sound to reach us, but from the absence of all sign of life I gathered that the Chippewas were resting after their terrific march. I felt none of the Mohawk's contempt for them; indeed, they seemed to me to be men to be reckoned with to the utmost, and as for Gib o' Clarclach, I had already experienced enough of his craft to know that he was no mean foe.

Toward midday I saw a number of dark forms appear to the westward, and as they drew near there came a faint barking of dogs down the wind. There were a scant half-dozen men in the arriving party, and the others turned out to meet them, after which all disappeared within the huts. Plainly, Gib considered that half a score men were enough to guard the western trail, which showed that it must be well-nigh impassable to Uchichak.

Then weariness came upon me, and I awoke Radisson, who yielded me his place beside the fire. Covering my head, I was soon fast asleep despite the cold, and when I woke again it was to find the day all but spent and The Keeper gone.

"Eat as little as may be, Davie," said Radisson as I warmed some of the frozen meat before the fire. "We have none too much to last us."

So I scarce touched the little supply of food. There was no more to be had unless we retraced our steps into the Barren Places, or descended into the forested basin to seek the game that must be plentiful there. Indeed, as I later learned, the place was thick with game, for the animals knew well that here they were safe from hunters.

The Keeper, it seemed, was scouting. I marvelled how the old chief could venture forth, but Radisson explained that the Chippewas seemed to keep but a slight watch, and for all my gazing I could see no signs of the Mohawk.

"How long, think you, ere Swift Arrow comes upon the Crees?"

Radisson shrugged his shoulders. "No telling, lad. He would not have gone through to the outside before noon at the earliest, and the dogs were sore spent. If he should chance upon them to the westward, he might be here by morning; but it may well be two or three days until their arrival. We must be far from the trail of The Pike."

This was scant consolation, and so we waited in silence. Still came no sign of The Keeper, and soon the Spirits of the Dead were dancing to the north, faintly. It must have been that age had dimmed the cunning of Radisson, for as I foolishly placed more wood on the fire, he made no comment. Suddenly from out of the darkness came a swift stream of words, angry and vehement, in the voice of The Keeper.

The result astonished me, for with one swift leap Radisson had sprung past me and was kicking the fire into embers over the snow. I was on my feet instantly, staring amazed at the tall figure of the chief.

"What is the matter? Surely our fire could not be seen from below?"

The Keeper grunted sarcastically. "Has my father lost his cunning? Has White Eagle been dreaming the dreams of women? From below the fire is hid, but the reflection of the fire was high on the cliffs."

Radisson, Indian-like, grunted disgustedly, and finished the last ember with his heel. But he said nothing, merely looking to the Mohawk inquiringly.

"There are two tens of men," reported the Keeper briefly. "The Pike is their chief. Their lodges are old. The Yellow Lily is there, also a woman of the Chippewas. One of their young men I met, gathering wood."

He touched his robes, as if beneath them lay something concealed. Radisson's words told me what that something was. The old man spoke quite as a matter of course.

"Then The Keeper will have another scalp to hang in the smoke of his lodge. Think you they saw the reflection of our fire?"

"I backed against the bowlder and shook them off, sending one sprawling with every blow."

The Mohawk shrugged his shoulders and made no reply. The two might have been discussing the weather or the stars for all the emotion they displayed, instead of the vital danger which threatened us all. And now I began to feel that the disdain expressed by the two Mohawks was not groundless. They were of another race than the chattering Crees and Chippewas. They seemed to hold themselves aloof, as if theirs was the heritage of more than these other men might comprehend. And truly I think it was, for there was in the whole bearing of The Keeper a great grimness, like unto the grimness of Fate, and at times since I have wondered if he could have seen some hint of what his end was to be.

We were now in darkness, save for the rising gleam of the fires in the sky. It seemed that Radisson and the Mohawk intended to wait until later in the night before they stole down to rescue Ruth. The cold was now intense, but despite my shiverings I saw that both Radisson and the Indian were listening to something that I could not hear. From the trees below rose a long wolf-howl, answered faintly by the voices of the Chippewa dogs.

"That was a poor cry, Keeper," and Radisson rose to his feet noiselessly. Then the snow crunched and crackled, and I saw the two slipping into the long shoes. One by one the guns were examined and primed afresh, and Radisson turned to me.

"We will steal down and wait, lad. Do you come to the crest of the ridge, there to cover our retreat if need be."

Picking up the extra guns, I donned my snowshoes and we stepped forth from the shelter of the niche in the cliffs. Out to the north the sky was just beginning to blaze in the spirit-dance, and the faint glimmer of light among the trees betokened a campfire, while behind us rose the gaunt, bleak cliffs. To right and left in a long curve swept the bare-blown, bowlder-strewn ridge, and for a moment we stood watching.

On a sudden The Keeper whirled about, and as he did so I heard a sharp, clear note behind. Something struck me and bounded away from my furs, and even as the whistle of another arrow rang past, Radisson had flung me from my feet. A gunshot split the night, and another, and one lone, weird yell rose up.

"Cover, Davie, cover!" cried Radisson, slipping behind a bowlder. The Mohawk had clean vanished, but his voice quavered out in a single soul-rending war-cry such as I had never heard before. Then, gun in hand, I was crouching beside Radisson.

"That was poor aiming," he muttered.

"They should have downed us at the first fire, or waited until—ah!"

Once more a musket spoke from the darkness, and the bullet crashed on the bowlder. Radisson fired instantly, then a choking cry came back to us. Now I realized that Gib had indeed seen our fire and with his cunning had surrounded us. Had he waited until daylight, we had never left that ridge alive, but doubtless the impatience of his warriors had overruled his craftiness.

"Wait here, lad," whispered Radisson as he reloaded, "while I seek The Keeper. We must not let daylight find us here."

If it did, it would find us frozen, I thought, while the arrows pattered around. No sign of any foe had I seen, but the blaze of the heavens began to light the dark face of the cliff as Radisson crawled away. Above, nestling against the face of the cliff, was a patch of drifted snow, and as my eyes grew accustomed to the light it seemed to me that across this a shadow moved.

I set my fusil in rest, and of a sudden my trembling hands grew firm again, as I drew a careful sight on that patch of snow. A shadow struck against it and wavered there, and in that instant I fired. While the long echoes of the shot died away on the farther cliffs, something crashed and was, silent.

Before I could withdraw the gun, an arrow pierced my fur sleeve and quivered loosely in my arm. I jerked it away, for the hurt was but slight, and reloaded. Then came a shot from somewhere to my left, and again that long, heart-splitting yell of the Mohawk shrilled up. It was answered by two sudden shots, and catching up one of the spare guns beside me I fired at the flashes.

This drew on me another shower of arrows, and a bullet that spat into the bowlder at my side and rebounded past my ear. This had come from behind, and with a sudden fear I turned. As I did so a yell that seemed to come from the throats of devils rang through the night, and I saw a number of dark forms leaping upon me. With swift terror in my heart, I sprang up, forgetting the fusils at my feet, and met them with clenched fists. I saw a pale glint of steel and struck out with all my strength, shouting aloud for Radisson. Then my fear dropped away from me as the first man went down beneath my fist, and I stepped forward, raging. The leaping, yelling demons seemed all about me, but I backed against the bowlder and shook them off, sending one sprawling with every blow. I caught the exultant voice of Gib, and leaped at a dark form ahead; catching him about the waist, I felt strength surge into me and heaved him high—then something came down on my head and I fell asleep with the sting of snow on my face.

CHAPTER XVI

A VOICE IN THE NIGHT

I KNEW NO more of what passed until I found myself lying on a pile of skins, my head throbbing painfully. Opening my eyes, I saw that I was lying beside a fire, while around me were Chippewas, and standing over me was my enemy.

"Awake, eh?" said Gib softly, in the old Gaelic, which he spoke with the Highland burr. There was an evil smile on his crafty face as I struggled to sit up. For a wonder, I was not bound, which I suppose he did not deem necessary.

"You are a troublous fighter, MacDonald," he sneered. "But with the great Radisson dead, you will have hard work to squeeze out of this pocket of mine."

"Radisson—dead?" I echoed dizzily. The shock of it cleared my head and I looked up at him. "You lie, Gib o'Clarclach! No dog such as you could slay Pierre Radisson! His fate lies in higher hands than yours!"

"So?" he snarled, sudden rage whelming in him. Swiftly, he reached out and kicked me with a vicious foot. I gathered myself together, but brown hands gripped me and held me there helpless, while he raved wildly in his madness. And by that I knew that he had lied, and that Radisson was not dead. So I laughed at him as they bound me hand and foot.

More than one of his men seemed wounded beneath their furs, and beside the fire lay two silent warriors. We were in the center of the group of lodges, and as there were but half a score of men around me. I gathered that the rest were scattered through the trees on watch. There was no sign of Ruth, and with that I set myself to taunt mine enemy, speaking in the Cree which all his men doubtless could understand.

"You are a fine leader of men, my brother! Well were you called The Pike—crafty, cowardly warrior who shuns the shallow water! See, in our village lies your chief Soan-ge-ta-ha, while our women laugh at him, and in the snow lies one of his young men, dead. The Cree knives are sharpened, my brothers, and with them are the knives of Radisson, the White Eagle, and of his friends, the Brothers of the Thunder." For this was the name by which the two Mohawks went in all that north country.

My words, as they were designed, sent a swirl of rage through the Chippewas, who with a growl turned on Gib. But he, the crafty one, appeased them swiftly.

"Brave Heart is not hurt, my brothers," he cried. "My medicine tells me that he is even now on his way to join us. As for you, Brave Eyes, you lie. The White Eagle has no men with him—only the tall Mohawk chief."

"Yes, mayhap," I answered, "but these twain are more than a match for your Chippewa women. You stole upon our village, and what gained you? Only one poor captive. It was a great raid, worthy of The Pike, and you have paid for it dearly with your chief and your young men. And the White Eagle is sharpening his claws, my brothers—out there in the night somewhere."

My words reached them, and more than my words. For barely had I finished, when the darkness was split asunder by a musket-shot. The man beside Gib whirled about and fell into the fire.

"Scatter!" foamed Gib, raging. "Scatter and slay the White Eagle, fools! Out with the fire!"

The embers were dashed over the snows instantly, and under his rapid orders the band vanished. Two of them remained to lift me, and they carried me to the door of one of the lodges, a little apart from the rest. Gib flung away the flap, and by the light of the lodge-fire inside I saw the pale, frightened face of Ruth.

"What means this intrusion?" she demanded in French, not seeing me. "I thought we were to remain unmolested!"

The scoundrel tendered her a low, mocking bow, and stepped aside to show my figure, as the two braves flung me at her feet. She gave but a little frighted cry, and stood facing him.

"A meeting of old friends, Mistress de Courbelles." It was the first time I had heard Ruth's name from other than the lips of Radisson. "How could I separate such dearly loved ones? See, I bring you a visitor of great value, and ere long you will have others. So I bid you good-even." With this he bowed again and was gone. Outside came his voice giving sharp orders, and all was still. But Ruth sprang forward and was on her knees beside me.

"My poor Davie!" she cried, lifting my head in her arms. "Some water, Laughing Snow!"

From out the shadows moved the figure of a Cree woman—a sister of Uchichak's, whom the Chippewas had carried away to care for Ruth. She brought water, and the two of them bathed my wounded head, where I had been struck down from behind. As they did so, I told them all that had passed.

"It was the night after you and The Crane left for the hunt," Ruth told me, "that the Chippewas came. For a little while the old men held them off, which gave most of the women time to flee. I had just left my lodge to find the cause of the shouting when Gib's party broke through. They seized me, set fire to the lodges, and were gone again. Oh, they treated me kindly enough, Davie, but—but I cannot bear that smiling, evil face of Gib!"

"Be not afraid, sister," spoke out the Cree woman, stolidly. "The Crane is a great warrior, and his men must be very near. These Chippewa women will flee before him like leaves before the wind of autumn."

"Yes, I think that Gib's plans were all upset by Brave Heart," I tried to reassure the little maid bravely enough. "But for him, and for the Mighty One, we had never been here, Ruth. As it is, the Swift Arrow will bring Uchichak and his men."

"We have been foolish," declared Laughing Snow bitterly. She went on to tell us how, years ago, it had been rumored that men lived in the Ghost Hills. By piecing together the fragments of Radisson's tales and this of hers, Ruth and I gathered that Gib o' Clarclach had maintained a sort of robber band in these dreaded hills in the old days, when French and English were at war on the Bay. Gib had afterwards, when Radisson dwelt in England, made the journey from the Canadas with d'Iberville and his raiders, and had guided them to the English posts when the French swept them clean. The villain had served both sides, lending himself wherever the more gain promised, and the Cree woman prophesied that once these things were known in the land, her people would make a war on the Chippewas that would go down in fable long afterwards. So indeed they did, but these things came in after years and have no part in this my tale.

There was little sleep for us that night. We had all rested during the day. I high on the ridge, and Ruth in the lodge, for the trip had been a hard one. The two women told how they had come through deep gorges, like those by which we had followed the Mighty One, and how they had given up all hope of rescue.

Now came something which has ever left a great wonder in my mind—one of those turns of chance which come in the most desperate straits. For, when my bonds had been removed, Ruth took from its skin wrappings a little book and showed it to me.

"I found this in the lodge," she said slowly. "Look upon the title-page, Davie, and see if I have been dreaming or not. It seems very hard to believe."

The book was a little leather-bound Bible. As the Cree woman put a flare of birch on the fire, I held it to the light and opened it. There in faded ink were words written, and I copy them from the Book which lies before me as I write. They were in the Dutch tongue, and as follows:

> "To Hendrik, to bear with him always in the desert places, that he may make straight in the wilderness a highway for our God. From his beloved wife. A.D. 1605."

And under this, in a firm writing that bespoke strength, were the English words, "Henry Hudson, his book." I stared again, scarce crediting the thing, then looked up to meet the grave, fearful eyes of Ruth. We had both heard the story many a time—how the bold sailor had been set adrift in an open boat, with his son and a few faithful ones, and how they had vanished. Just a century since, 1610, had this thing taken place, and no word had ever come to England of Henry Hudson, through all the years between.

"Then," I almost whispered, "think you that this was really his? How came it here?"

"It speaks for itself," and Ruth dropped beside me and fingered the Book reverently. "Think of it, Davie! In the midst of the wilderness, in the midst of foes, to come into an empty lodge and find this thing! Does it not seem like a message of faith and hope?"

"As to that," I responded, "like enough. But I was thinking on the marvel of it, Ruth. It must even be that Hudson, who was thought to have perished in the waters of the Great Bay, escaped to land. Else how could this Bible have come here? How could Gib have obtained it? Perhaps from the Indians."

With this I turned to Laughing Snow and questioned her closely. But she disclaimed all knowledge of the Book, and said that never before the coming of Radisson had white faces been seen in the northern lands.

For a time we discussed the wonder, failing to gain any information from the Cree woman, but my bandaged head hurt painfully, and after the first surprise I leaned back, faint and weak. Then Ruth took the little volume, warped and stained with time and sea-water, and read to us aloud. As she read, she translated into Cree for the benefit of the other.

I was quite content to lie silently and gaze at her. Very beautiful she seemed there in the faint fire-glow, which tinged her golden hair with ruddy hues and likened her grave, sweet face with the rise and fall of the flames. Her heavy beaver-skins were laid aside, and her inner dress of soft doeskin was decorated with the beautifully marked neck-skins of loons, which Radisson had brought her. Porcupine quills and shell beads fringed her moccasins, while at her throat gleamed that same little gold brooch which had led us so far and brought upon us so much trouble.

Through all our journeys I had kept by me that stained and torn fragment of my father's Bible, and when she had done I wrapped it up again in the skin with the volume that had been Henry Hudson's, and gave them into the keeping of Ruth. Barely had we settled back when the skin flap was pushed aside, and once more Gib o' Clarclach entered.

"I would have some speech with you, David," he announced, no longer smiling, but purposeful and shrewd. Closing the door to keep out the cold, he seated himself on some skins and stared at me across the fire. I made him no answer.

"My young friend, these Chippewas of mine, I keenly regret, are not used to the customs of civilized war. Yet they are far ahead of your Mohawk friends, whom I have seen tie their captives to a tree and build a fire round about. These Chippewas have another method, which is quite as effective; for instead of a fire, they shoot arrows until the victim is like a porcupine with his quills erect. Then they shoot for the heart."

"Well, have on your murderers," I replied, knowing well that he dared not for the sake of Soan-ge-ta-ha. "Methinks their chief will suffer if I do."

"That is exactly the trouble, my bold young friend," he answered me. "Personally, it matters little to me what becomes of the chief, for he disobeyed my orders. But his warriors take another view of the situation. They would have me be fool enough to turn you loose so that their chief may be restored to them."

"Then they may save their worry," I shot back bluntly enough. "If you want Brave Heart, give the maid here back."

"Ah, that is impossible," his suave answer irritated me the more. "For her, we are to receive many fine gifts at the Post—beads and powder and blankets and—other things. No, I deeply regret that I am unable to meet your just demand. But on the other hand, as I was about to propose, unless you consent to parley with Radisson for the return of the chief, my warriors will insist on using you as a target."

Ruth stared at him with frighted eyes, but I knew well enough that the man spoke in deadly earnest. Could I have had my way of it, I would have bade him do his worst; but a little hand fluttered down to my wrist, and I could not withstand the unspoken appeal of Ruth.

"Have it your own way, then," I growled. "I suppose you would have me seek my friends at once?"

"Not till the day, sweet sir," smiled the scoundrel. "My men are all about, and there is no danger of your two or three eager friends inflicting any more damage. I do not quite understand how you got in here, unless you were hunting—no, that could not be either."

He fell to musing, staring at me, whereat I laughed harshly.

"It was no hand of man led us here, Gib o' Clarclach, make sure of that."

"Then we will even ascribe it to the foul fiend," and he got to his feet. "Good-even for the last time, mistress!"

When he had gone we sat silent, all three. Presently the Cree woman fell asleep in her corner and the fire slowly died down to a dim red glow, while Ruth and I sat hand in hand. On the morrow, it seemed like, I would go forth and bargain for my worthless skin, leaving her in the hands of our enemies. Bitterly I cursed myself for a faint-heart, though I knew full well that ere long Uchichak and his warriors would turn the tide of affairs.

The long hours passed, and still I sat sleepless, Ruth having fallen half into slumber, her head resting against my shoulder. I was staring at the skin wall of the lodge, where it was lashed into the brush beyond, and was dreaming again of that terrible voyage and of its ending, when I started suddenly. The glow of the embers had seemed to strike a spark from the wall—a tiny point of light that moved across the skin!

In a moment I knew it was a knife-blade slitting the tough hide, whereat I brought Ruth wide awake. The skin seemed to fall apart in silence, and through it glared a horrible painted mask and staring eyes. Ruth clutched my arm, in fright, but a whisper came from the darkness.

"Brave Eyes! Come swiftly!" And I knew it for the voice of The Keeper.

CHAPTER XVII

A MARTYR OF THE SNOWS

IT WAS Ruth who woke me from my stupid amazement, pushing me to my feet as The Keeper whispered again. How that crafty Mohawk had pierced the ring of Chippewas, I never knew, but his forest skill must have been far beyond theirs. I remembered the little buckskin bag of paint which always hung at his girdle, and knew that he must have prepared himself according to his own custom.

But my wits came back to me quickly enough, and I pushed Ruth forward to the opening, first stamping out the embers lest they betray us. As quietly as might be I helped her through the narrow slit, the Mohawk receiving us on the other side, and Grim following. Then we were standing in the shelter of a small fir, and for a wonder the skies were dark save for the eternal stars. I looked about for Radisson, but he was not to be seen.

"Come!" breathed The Keeper, leading the way through the snow. None of us wore snowshoes, but the crust was firm enough to support us, with the intense cold of those nights. There was no sound around us save the crackle of the frost as the trees creaked in the wind, nor was any fire visible.

Yet I knew that all about us were men watching and listening. It seemed hardly possible that we should win through to the ridge where I supposed that Radisson waited, but gradually we left the camp behind. Once we were beyond the circle of trees would come the danger, although the absence of the lights seemed to protect us somewhat. We went cautiously and slowly, and it must have been fifteen minutes before the trees thinned out around us.

Then, without warning, a sudden streamer of flame quivered and hung across the skies, and the lights were dancing, lighting up all things in grotesque shadow-gleams. I knew we were lost, even before a dark form bounded into the snow before us and a shrill yell went up that echoed across the night.

"Go!" exclaimed The Keeper in French, pushing Ruth ahead. "Run to the crest yonder, where White Eagle waits!" I sent Grim with a quick word also.

Ruth, with a little sobbing cry, obeyed, and the Mohawk flung himself in one great leap on the figure which was coming toward us. Steel flashed in the half-light and the two went down together. But other forms were yelling at our heels, and if Ruth was to be saved this was no time to run. We must hold them back for a moment or two.

The Keeper rose swiftly and put into my hand the heavy stone ax he had taken from the Chippewa. Then, gripping knife in one hand and tomahawk in the other, he waited at my side as the warriors came at us. Glancing around, I saw Ruth's dark figure vanishing over the snows toward the ridge; as I later learned, she thought we were close behind her, else had she never deserted us.

"Now, brother!" grunted The Keeper. "Back to back!"

With a swirl of snow the dark figures were on us. But the yells of rage turned to warning cries as that huge ax of mine swung up and down, and the lithe Mohawk used his two hands with the swiftness of a panther. They drew back, then came at us again; this time I knew the form of The Pike for their leader, and sprang out to meet him with my ax whirled aloft.

He avoided my stroke, leaping aside and stooping in the snow. Ere I could fathom his intent the others were upon me, pressing me back to the side of the Mohawk. They shrank before that crashing ax and swift tomahawk, and with each blow I caught an approving grunt from the old warrior beside me. We

were ringed about with dark forms in the snow, silent and
motionless, when I caught sight of Gib again.

Too late, I saw his aim. He had broken off a huge section of
the snow-crust, and as I turned to meet him he flung the mass
in my face, blinding me and sending me staggering. In vain did
I strike out blindly, for hands gripped my throat and bore me
back fighting furiously into the snow. I heard a single long yell
from The Keeper, and as I went down saw a gleam of light dart
from his hand. The tomahawk whirled into one of the men who
gripped me, but it was of no avail. I was choked into helplessness and when something hit my wounded head, I knew no
more.

Once again I wakened to find myself lying beside a fire, but
now it was the broad daylight. My head scarcely pained, though
my throat was sore where I had been gripped, and I was fast
bound. With a turn of the head it was easy to see all that lay
around.

At my side was The Keeper, in similar plight to mine, though
his face seemed old and gray and sunken and his furs were red
with frozen blood. He lay quiet, his eyes closed, but the sudden
fear that he was dead departed when I saw the rise and fall of
his breast. His painted face was hideous, yet could not mask
the age and weakness and strength of the man; weak he was in
body, wounded and spent, but his spirit was as strong as that
of Pierre Radisson himself.

Sullen and cursing, the Chippewas were grouped about the
fire. More than one of them lay helpless, or with rude-bandaged
wounds, and all were eying the Mohawk and me with malignant
ferocity. But Ruth was uppermost in my mind. Had she been
saved? Or had The Keeper's sacrifice been vain?

Guessing from the sun, it was early morning. I looked across
and up to the ridge of cliffs, and imagined that I could see a
thin trail of smoke ascending. Whether it were my imagination
or no, I could not tell for sure: still, the thought cheered me. At

the least, Radisson must be safe, and of Ruth I would soon learn.

But the time dragged on, and by midday intolerable thirst consumed me. The Mohawk had by now come out of his swoon, and lay staring straight up into the sky, nor did I venture to bespeak him. Presently there was a stir about the fire, and from one of the lodges came Gib. Then he entered that wherein Ruth and I had lain, and came back to us with that little skin package which we had forgot in the haste of our flight. He unrolled it and laughed shortly. At a curt order from him The Keeper and I were brought up sitting, against a small hemlock. But when Gib had come to that torn cover of my father's Bible, his face changed horribly, and he flung the whole from him as if it burnt his hands—as very possibly it did.

"So, dog of an Iroquois," he snarled at The Keeper, his features convulsed with rage, "it is you whom I have to thank for the loss of men and captive, eh? *Mort de ma vie!* But you shall suffer for this, and speedily!"

So he raged, cursing in French, Gaelic and a dozen more tongues, while the Chippewas silently and grimly made ready their arrows and bows.

"You, MacDonald," went on Gib at length, "shall see what your fate will be if Brave Heart be not returned to us safe. As for the girl, I shall have her in the end—and would have her back here ere this, but there is no place she can flee to, and my men are athirst for revenge."

From which I judged shrewdly enough that the Chippewas had refused to face the fire of Radisson from the ridge, after my fall, and that Ruth had escaped to him. This was mightily cheering, and now I cared not what took place, since the little maid was safe.

At word from Gib, two or three of the Chippewas sprang forward and pulled The Keeper to his feet, loosing his bonds and mine and casting off his furs until he stood naked to the waist. The old warrior was scarred with new wounds and old,

*"Still holding the book, the old Mohawk answered
slowly, unheeding the bitter cold in his fresh wounds."*

and I judged that he had not gone down in last night's struggle
without giving more than one deathblow. His sinewy bronze
figure drew a look of admiration from the surrounding warriors,
and when the power of movement was restored to him he
quietly leaned over and picked up the little Bible which had
been Henry Hudson's.

"So," sneered Gib at this, noting also the emblem of the Cross that hung around the neck of the old Mohawk, "you are of the faith of the blackrobes, Iroquois? Say, will you not accept life and a chieftainship among the Chippewas?"

Before The Keeper could reply to the Cree words, one of the other warriors stepped forth and spoke in the same tongue.

"Old man, you are a brave warrior. Last night you fought well. Beside the fire lies my older brother. His squaw will mourn for him. You shall take his place at our councils, and be a chief among us."

Quiet scorn flashed into the proud, haggard face of the old man, but he said no word, and once again Gib taunted him with his creed.

"Give up that thing about your neck, Iroquois, fling that book into the snow, and you shall be a great man among us and saved from the torture. How say you? What avails your faith now? Is it stronger than Chippewa arrows? Can it break the Chippewa bows?"

The Keeper turned and faced him. Into the stern old features had crept a light that seemed unearthly, and he looked at Gib as though he had seen some other behind him, so that more than one of the warriors glanced about uneasily. Still holding the Book, the old Mohawk answered slowly, unheeding the bitter cold in his fresh wounds.

"The Pike is a great warrior. He was among the Iroquois many years ago. He has seen how warriors of the Five Nations die, and the sight has frightened him. He has fled to the Chippewas, and has put on the robes of a squaw. He asks me, the Keeper of the Eastern Door of the Long-house. Ta-cha-noon-tia, if my faith is stronger than Chippewa arrows! Listen, my brothers.

"I am very old. I am on my last war-trail, and I can see that it is almost ended, and I am glad. But in the snow beside The Pike there is a trail. What is that which stands behind you, my brother? What is that which waits at your shoulder and breathes upon your cheek?"

At the words Gib, who had listened as though through force, flung about, but there was no man beside him. Then from the Chippewas went up a little gasp, and following their eyes I saw a track across the snow, from the woods leading toward the ridge, which passed close to us and right behind Gib. The track was that of the Mighty One, the giant moose, and I realized that The Keeper was taking advantage of every chance that offered.

But Gib laughed harshly. "The Keeper is right. He is on his last trail, unless he casts away the book in his hand, and quickly."

"Listen, my brothers, while I tell you a story." At this I saw Gib start as if to protest, but a swift glance at the Chippewas showed that he could not hurry them. They were absorbed in watching The Keeper, and although their admiration for him would in no degree lessen their cruelty, they wished to lose nothing of his words or deeds, for they knew that he was a greater man than they. He spoke slowly, quietly, his weak voice growing stronger as he went on.

"Long ago, when I was a young warrior without a scalp, a man came among us. He wore a black robe. He was a white man, and his words were sweet in our ears. He told us that the Great Spirit had sent him among us to tell us that there should be peace and not war in the land.

"My brothers, our old men have told us that once the hero Hiawatha banded together five nations in a silver chain of peace. These are the five nations of the Iroquois. No tribe can stand before us—not even the white men have overcome us. But we have forgotten that we formed a league of peace, and our arrows are very sharp.

"We listened to the blackrobe, but we did not believe that the Great Spirit had sent him to us. Our medicine men were very angry at him. Then there came a plague upon us, and many of our warriors died in the villages. The medicine men said that the blackrobe had brought the plague upon us, and our young men cried out that he should be killed.

"My brothers, you do not know how to torture. You are women. We took the blackrobe to a stake and builded a fire around him. Before we lit the fire I jeered at him, and asked him if his Great Spirit was stronger than our arrows, stronger than our fire."

There was dead silence, for The Keeper was holding his audience by the sheer force of his words, and the Chippewas were wrapt in his story.

"My brothers, he answered that his faith was greater than our fire or our tomahawks. We were very glad, for we knew that he would die like a warrior. I myself set the fire around him, but he seemed to feel no pain. He gazed up at the sky and spoke to the Great Spirit as the coals fell upon him, so that we became afraid. And, my brothers, before he died we heard him ask the Great Spirit to bless us and not to take vengeance upon us. Then in truth we knew that his faith was greater than our fire, and that his Great Spirit had blunted our arrows. In the next year I went to seek out the White Father, and there I learned to know the Great Spirit, and I placed his token about my neck.

"My brothers, you have heard my story. You have asked me to deny the Great Spirit, but He has whispered to me that He is stronger than your bows and sharper than your arrows. I am sore wounded, and the end of the trail appears before me, my brothers. I have killed many of your young men, who shall journey with me on the ghost-trail to find the Great Spirit. And when I find Him I will ask him to bless you.

"Brave Eyes," and for an instant the stern voice faltered, as The Keeper turned to me, "carry this book to White Eagle, my father, and tell him that the Chippewas are women. Tell him that Ta-cha-noon-tia was a great warrior, and that I will wait for him on the Ghost-trail. Tell the Great Swift Arrow, my brother, that I will wait for him also. Tell them that we have traveled long together, and that the Great Spirit has whispered to me that He will not separate us for long. My brothers, I have spoken."

Handing the Bible to me, The Keeper turned and folded his arms calmly. For a moment the Chippewas were held under the spell of his words, then a word from Gib wakened them. With all respect they led The Keeper to a large tree outside the lodges, and bound him fast.

But as for me, I buried my head in my arms, and sobbed— great, dry, choking sobs that I could by no means check nor hinder, and cared not who saw them. For I was alone and helpless, and the bitter agony in my heart was well-nigh unendurable.

So passed Ta-cha-noon-tia, the Keeper of the Eastern Door—and never in all the North was there a passing which so truly deserved the name of martyrdom.

CHAPTER XVIII

HUDSON'S END

I DO NOT think that this triumph of The Pike was greatly to his liking, after all. That speech of The Keeper had staggered him, and I caught him more than once, in the hours that followed, gazing steadfastly at the track of the Mighty One across the snows. How that track came there I know not; the moose must have passed from the forest to the ridge during the night without being seen or heard, which was like enough.

So I sat there alone, my head upon my arms, until the thudding of the arrows had ceased and a single yell from the Chippewas told me that it was finished. No word or groan had the Mohawk uttered, and the warriors laid him down beside their own dead and covered him with his robes in silent respect.

Gib had stood, at my side, watching in stony silence all that passed, and at the end he turned and strode away, entering one of the lodges. The Chippewas left me to myself, hovering near and conversing in low tones. The death of the martyr had cast a gloom over the day, and I saw the Cree woman, Laughing Snow, moving about among the lodges. For some reason she had not accompanied us in that mad flight, but I spared little thought on her. I was too full of my grief and rage, for him who had died.

So dragged away an hour or two. Then Gib reappeared and said somewhat to his men, who bestirred themselves promptly. I gathered that with the first darkness they would make an attack on Radisson to recover Ruth from him, and misdoubted me much that he could hold the ridge single-handed, or even the pass itself. It was not to be altogether as Gib had planned, however, for before the afternoon had gone a murmur of amazement from the Chippewas awoke me from my lethargy. Glancing up, I saw a single figure advancing over the snows from the ridge. Halting midway to us, it stopped and held up both hands, and I recognized Radisson.

Now, at the time, there were only some eight or nine warriors in camp, the others having gone forth at Gib's command to bring in some fresh meat. Had the others been here, that which took place had been next to impossible. Gib strode out and shouted to Radisson to come forward without fear, assuring him of safety, then he turned back with a swift word.

"Bind that white man's hands and gag him," was his order, and the Chippewas obeyed. In a moment I was trussed and gagged, while Gib flung another blanket over the still form of The Keeper. That he was up to some deviltry I guessed, but could not fathom his purpose.

Radisson slapped along over the snows, and presently came up to us. He was unarmed, and as he paused I could see his keen eyes searching as if for someone who was not visible. It took no great thought to guess who that someone was, and I thought he looked puzzled.

"Greetings, my brothers," he said courteously enough, paying no heed to me, but striding to the fire and warming himself. The Chippewas replied in kind, and Gib smiled craftily.

"Has White Eagle come to surrender, himself?" returned the renegade softly.

Radisson smiled. "Nay, but to demand surrender," was his cool retort, and he turned to the Chippewas, disdaining to speak with Gib. "My brothers, the end is near. The Great Spirit is fighting against you. See, he has led me through the hills by a secret path, and there on the ridge are gathered the Cree warriors. They were very eager to send their arrows to you, and I cannot restrain them much longer."

This created a little stir among the Chippewas, but still Gib smiled his sneering smile.

"My brothers, last night you captured Brave Eyes and one of the Brothers of the Thunder. The Yellow Lily was drooping in your hands, and she has fled to us. If I let loose my warriors upon you, they will eat you up and stamp you into the earth as the herds of bison stamp the grass. But return me your prisoners, and we will go in peace."

My heart gave a bound of joy. So the Crees had arrived with Swift Arrow! But Gib replied calmly enough.

"White Eagle, I am not like the fool Englishmen whom you captured in their forts single-handed in years past. I have not seen your young men, or heard the sound of their war cries."

Radisson turned and pointed out toward the westering sun that was turning the snow and hills and trees to crimson and purple. A guttural exclamation rose from the warriors, and Gib's smile faded away; for there we saw plainly a dozen dark figures wending toward us and dark against the sun.

"Your road to the west is cut off," continued Radisson. "Your escape is impossible. The warriors of Talking Owl have gathered against you, and if you would not be overwhelmed at once, you must act quickly. These young men come to join us, and there are others behind them. Say, my brothers, will you release your captives or no?"

Beneath the stolid calm of the Chippewas it needed no sharp eye to see that they were wild with fear. Gib's cunning tongue had failed him for once, and he could naught but gaze out at the little dots against the sun. They were still a mile or more away, and to detect more than that they were men was impossible. In that moment it seemed that Radisson had triumphed utterly, and the oldest of the Chippewas nodded gravely.

"My father White Eagle is a great warrior. If he will assure us that these men will do us no harm, will let us go in peace, and if he will not bring the warriors of Uchichak upon us, then he may take his captives. But Brave Heart must also be released."

"So it shall be," and I detected nothing of the anxiety that must have underlain Radisson's calm demeanor. "These men shall not harm you, my brothers, and those who are with me shall not attack you. Soan-ge-ta-ha shall return home in safety." Gib started to utter a bitter protest, but the Chippewas waved him into silence, and pulled me to my feet, shoving me forward to Radisson. He drew out his knife to cut my bonds, and asked after The Keeper. It was Gib who made answer, accepting the situation.

"The Mohawk is out with some of our young men, Radisson. He will be back shortly, and he shall join you then. Brave Eyes must remain as he is, lest he attack us, for he is strong."

For an instant Radisson hesitated, and a swift flash of disappointment ran over his stern face. Then it came to me that he must have played a desperate game, and vainly I strove to warn him. The flimsy excuses of the renegade seemed to be accepted, however, for without a word he stepped forward and led me away, none hindering.

When we had gone a hundred yards, from the camp he whipped out his knife, gave one quick glance to the west, and cut through my bonds.

"Run for it, lad!" he cried. "Some of the Chippewa hunters have met the others—we are lost unless we break away to the ridge!"

I did not pause to question him, but ran. For a moment I thought we would be safe enough, but the Chippewas must have been watching that party to the west also, for we had barely started when from the camp behind went up a shrill yell of rage, and I heard Gib's shout.

I knew without his telling me that he had tried for one of those audacious coups which had made his name famous, even as Gib had said. The Crees had not arrived; the party to the west was the party of the Chippewas who had been left to guard the retreat, and who for some reason had come on to join Gib.

Had the hunters from the camp not met them, in plain sight of all, we had got clean away.

As it was, I was handicapped by having no snowshoes, but even so I could outrun the Chippewas, as I knew well. Then something whistled over my shoulder, and a gunshot rang out behind us, and another. Those Chippewas were well armed, doubtless from the post, and in their rage at being tricked so easily they spared no powder.

I dared not try to jump from side to side, nor could Radisson by reason of his snowshoes, so we plunged straight for the ridge. The bullets whistled past us and over, and I had just begun to rejoice that we had escaped, when I saw Radisson stagger heavily. Then came wild fear to me, and I reached his side and caught his arm in mine.

" 'Tis naught, Davie," he muttered as he ran on, and shook me off, "have distanced them—courage! Where is The Keeper?"

Before answering I glanced behind. The Chippewas had spread out, but were making no further effort to catch us. Another spurt of smoke darted out, and another bullet sang past faintly. A hundred yards farther on and we would be out of range, so I waited until we had gained it, with the ridge near ahead.

"The Keeper is dead." I answered him bluntly enough. "They shot him to death with arrows at midday."

Radisson stopped short and turned a stricken face to me. Terrible was that face, unbelieving my tidings, yet with fear and horror stamped upon it. The old man staggered as he stood, swaying back and forth, but his eagle-eyes were never brighter and keener.

"Dead? The Keeper dead?" he repeated hoarsely. In a few words I told him all that had passed. He bowed his head slowly, and two great tears trickled down over his beard, but no more. When he raised his countenance again I scarce knew it, so deep-sunken was it all in a moment, so ghastly pale.

"Come, Davie," he muttered as if his spirit had broken beneath the weight of sorrow. "Swift Arrow has not yet arrived. We are in bad case, and—and—I am hard hit."

I caught him with a cry of grief, but he gathered himself together and once more we went on. My mind was in a whirl, for I knew the old man was wounded and badly, yet I was thinking more of his terrible grief than of his wound. And so we came to the ridge again, and when we reached bare rock Ruth sprang forward and into my arms, Grim leaping up on me.

"Davie—Davie!" she cried, sobbing, then lifted her face to mine. I held her for an instant, and kissed her on the brow. But as I looked across her shoulder to Radisson I bethought me that he was hurt, and so I loosed her again and would have gone to him, but he stopped me.

"Listen, David! My strength is sore spent—we must leave this cranny in the rocks for the mouth of the pass, for with the darkness the Chippewas will be upon us. Stop not for talking, lad, but catch up the muskets and powder and hasten!" he said.

Seeing that it was useless to irritate him by not obeying, I loaded myself with the weapons and horns of powder, Ruth helping me bind on my snowshoes. Radisson stood, swaying a little, but gazing at the rock walls above as if searching for aid. We set out, Ruth at his arm, and wended beneath the cliffs toward the mouth of that valley of shadow through which we had come hither, striking a path through the great bowlders strewed around while Grim followed sedately. I cast watchful glances down toward the camp, but Gib seemed to be waiting for his hunters and for that second party before he moved on us. On a sudden the old wanderer paused, and his voice rang out as firm as ever.

"Look! The Mighty One has come again to lead us!"

And there in the snow were the tracks of that gigantic moose, fresh and new-made, and leading toward the mouth of the valley! We followed them as speedily as might be, and in ten minutes more the great rock walls had towered above and closed us in. Ruth had come to my side now, and she pressed close to me in fear.

The track suddenly turned away from those old tracks of ours, to one side of the rocks. Without hesitation Radisson followed, until we came to where the moose had milled around and around in the snow, possibly to make a bed—but as Radisson firmly believed, to point us to something. And great fear came upon me when Ruth gave a little cry and showed a long, narrow cleft in the black rocks at our side.

"Said I not that he was leading us?" cried Radisson triumphantly. "It is a cave, lad! There we can stand off the Chippewas as long as need be. Forward!"

I took out flint and steel, kindled my tinder, and presently had a roll of birch flaring. Above stretched that cleft in the granite, silent, black, grim with unseen terrors. I led the way gingerly enough, for the passage seemed to zigzag before me, as if some giant hand had smitten into the heart of the cliffs.

Then I paused abruptly, holding my flare high, as the passage opened out. Surely, it was a cave—small, but large enough to hold us in comfort. The room was a dozen feet across and at my feet lay a little store of wood as if someone else had been there, while skins were piled in the corner. My torch sputtered, and I swiftly lit the pile of sticks, which flared up instantly, flickering in a draught. Then at the far end of the chamber I saw a second opening, smaller than the first, and clad in darkness.

"We have an hour," muttered Radisson thickly, as he sank down upon the skins. "What is this place?"

"Let us tend your wound first," I besought him, whereat Ruth gave a little cry and came to his side.

"Oh, are you hurt?" she exclaimed softly, catching his head as he sank back, "is The Keeper?"

"He has gone before me," returned Radisson with more strength. "Nay, let be, lass. You can do me no good now, for I have come to the end of the trail. Eat of the food that is left, both of you; we will have need of all your strength ere morning, lad."

We obeyed him, while Ruth heard the story of The Keeper's passing, and wept as she ate until the tears choked her. Radisson spoke, dry-eyed and smiling, with Grim curled at his side.

"Lad, see what lies in that farther chamber, for it has taken strong hold on my mind."

Willing to humor him, I caught up a burning stick and went to the entrance, which was about mine own height. All was dark beyond, until I turned a sharp corner of the rock. I near dropped the light, and my heart leaped in fear, for a great bearded face was staring out upon me! Then I knew all.

Staring from across a rude table where it sat, was the figure of a man—in one hand an ancient pistol, in the other a quill, with paper before it. Upon the table sat a keg, with the word "Hudson" painted on it, and I needed not to look at that high brow encased in the frozen drippings from the rock above, to know that here had been the ending of Henry Hudson.

"**W**HAT IS it, Davie?" called the soft voice of Ruth, awaking me from my horrified stupor.

"Wait," I made hoarse answer, still dazed by my startling discovery. Looking closer at that figure before me, I saw that it was as if cased in ice, and as something splashed on my neck I knew that the rock-drippings from above had covered it. With trembling fingers I wiped the sweat from my brow, then caught at the sheet of paper before me and incontinently fled.

The horror of it unnerved me, and must have shown in my face. Gradually I told the others of what I had seen, and Radisson started up on his elbow, his old face alight with a great amazement and joy.

"The paper, lad—the paper!" he cried out. "Hendrik Hudson—ah, but this is the greatest discovery of all! Naught matters now—for I have goodly company on the Ghost-trail! Read the paper, lad!"

I held down the dry paper—for it seemed to have escaped those drippings, by some trick of Fate—to the light, and with Ruth peering over my shoulder made shift to read the words written there in English. It was in the same hand which had written in the Bible, and the two lie here before me now. It seemed to be one of other sheets, for at the top it was numbered in Roman.

"XI

shall beeware how you doe deal my Truste. In Time shall

come Them of mine own Race, to whom doe I graunt all thyngs Herein. This bee a rich laund & worthe ye keeping for Britain. Soe now farewell. I grow weak.

Henry Hudson."

I looked up from the paper amazed, and met the exultant eyes of Radisson fixed upon me. The old man clutched at the scrap and held it to him fiercely.

"Radisson has won again!" he exclaimed, his dark eyes shining bright. "I have found a new country and with it Henry Hudson—ah, get you outside, lad! Take the fusils with you, and keep guard! I had forgot our danger, and the night must be coming on. They will trail us here, for The Pike must know the place. Yet it is strange that he knew naught of the passage through the hills behind!"

So I loaded the fusils afresh and left him in the care of Ruth. When I gained the entrance to the cave I saw that it must have fallen dark outside, yet the mouth of the passage from the ridge was lit by the fires in the sky, which seemed faintly ablaze. As I set down the guns and drew my furs about me, shivering in the bitterness of the cold, I was thankful that at least I was sheltered from that great wind that tore down through the gap moaning and shrieking.

Where had that moose-track come from? It seemed hard to believe that the mighty animal had passed from woods to ridge, and so on into the passage without having been seen by any. Yet it must have been even so, for the trail was a fresh one, and I wondered at the thing.

With it all I was mightily afraid, nor hesitated to admit it to myself. The death of The Keeper had been a great shock to me, and the finding of Hudson, the mere knowing that his earthly form lay in that cave behind me, was horrible. The fearsomeness of that passageway through the cliffs, lying so dark and ghostly in front of me, added in no small degree to my shakings of soul.

And to cap all, Radisson lay stricken mortally. This I guessed from his manner of speaking and from the fact that he would not allow us to care for his wound. The great wonder of the whole thing, from the trail of the Mighty One to the martyrdom of the Mohawk, oppressed me, and I remembered how The Keeper had prophesied that he would not go on the spirit-trail alone.

Then I fell to thinking of Hudson. So the little boat had not been lost, as all men had thought, but had reached land. Who might know the tale of all that had happened? The stout seaman must have seen his friends and his son perish one by one, yet have struggled on to the west until he had come to the Ghost Hills and found there the rest denied him in life.

So I sat there half in dream, thinking bitterly on what was to be the end of it all. For myself I cared little, but I could not see Ruth in red hands. Why did not Swift Arrow and Uchichak arrive? Almost on the thought, it seemed that a dark shadow flitted down through the pass, whereat I caught up one of the guns and cried out.

"It is Ca-yen-gui-ha-no," came the voice of the Mohawk. "Where is my brother?"

"Here," I shouted, great relief in my heart, and had like to fling my arms about the tall old man as he clambered up to me. "But Uchichak—where are the Crees? We are in sore need, Swift Arrow!"

"They come," he grunted in surprise as he saw where I stood. "The Mighty One met us. I fired and drove him back. The Crees are slow. Swift Arrow came on quickly, and passed the Mighty One, who follows behind me."

He peered about, and I motioned him back into the cave, whither he vanished. A moment later there came a yell from the mouth of the gap, and I knew that the Chippewas were upon me. A number of dark shapes flitted across the opening, a hundred paces away, and I fired at one of these, the echoes rolling up and up in weird echoes of sound.

"Let my brother load," and Swift Arrow stood beside me again. "I will shoot."

Cheerfully enough I resigned my place to him. Now came two shots, and the bullets pattered on the cliffs behind. But to reach us the Chippewas would have to cross that open gully where lay the deep, hard snow, and even in the half-light from the closed-out skies their figures would show plainly against the white snow. And we had four guns, with a good store of powder and balls close to hand.

After those first shots, there came no sign of danger, but I knew that the cunning brain of The Pike would not rest idle for long. The Chippewas could not reach us from below without making a straight charge, which they would have little stomach for, and they could not get at us from above, since those high walls of granite could hardly be scaled.

Yet Gib solved the problem, for presently a musket roared over against us on the opposite side of the cliffs, and a bullet whistled into the cleft behind. There was no danger that those within the cavern could be injured, by reason of the twists in the passage, but the mouth of the cave where we lay could be raked easily enough, and the Arrow grunted.

"We must hit or be hit, Brave Eyes," and he laid his fusil in rest, aiming at the place whence had come the flash. A moment later it came again, but the Arrow fired almost with it. A single yell echoed up, and thereafter came no more shots from across the way.

"Think you they will try to rush upon us?" I whispered fearfully.

"They are women," he grunted disdainfully. "The Mighty One will scatter them."

"How mean you? Where is the moose?"

"He is near. The Crane will drive him before, and when he comes the Chippewas will scatter from before him."

Then I remembered what the Mohawk had first said, upon his arrival. He had met the moose traveling toward the open country, and had driven him back toward us, passing him later as he hurried on ahead of the Crees. But soon I had other things to bother my head with than the moose.

For as we lay watching, something came down from the skies and shattered on the rocks beside me. Feeling about, I found that it had been an arrow, and now we were in grave danger indeed. If we withdrew under the shelter of the cave, we would lose sight of that open gully beneath us; but if we lay there without covering above, the Chippewa arrows could descend full upon us. Gib was having his men shoot straight up, so that the arrows would fall with fearful force, and against such shooting we were defenseless.

They pattered down all around, shattering on the rock and yet seeming to miss us altogether. Before long the Mohawk, who had refused to listen to my word that we should seek shelter inside the cave and defend its mouth, began to chant something in a low voice that swelled louder and louder. A wild, barbaric chant it was, in words that I knew not, but ever and anon he would lift one of the fusils and shoot, though I could see no object at which to aim. When his chant died down again I asked him the meaning of it.

"I go on the Ghost-trail, my brother," he responded after a moment. "The Chippewa arrows are very sharp, and the Great Spirit has called me. I hear the voice of the Keeper of the Eastern Door. He asks me why I wait. I am waiting for my father the White Eagle, oh Ta-cha-noon-tia!" With which he trailed off into his own tongue once more and paid no further heed to me.

I knew not whether he had been struck with one of those falling arrows, for he had made no sign. A moment later he pressed a fusil into my hands.

"They come, brother! Be ready!"

I loaded it as rapidly as might be, but had not finished when a great yell went up from the darkness, and across the snow came the Chippewas—dark splotches that seemed to leap over the white ground.

The Arrow waited, and then when they seemed to be almost upon us, he began firing. One after another of the foremost figures went down, and I managed to get the first gun to him as he fired the fourth. Before that rain of lead the Chippewas broke and fled, but I heard the voice of Gib ring out, and knew that he was still unharmed. When the muskets were once more loaded, I left the ledge for an instant, and ran back to the cave, in order to reassure Ruth. I found her and Radisson just as I had left them, on the pile of skins, and although the fire had died down, there was plenty of wood in the cave from which to replenish it. In a few words I told them of the repulse.

"And Swift Arrow?" demanded Radisson quickly. "Why was he singing the death-chant? Is he also hurt?"

"I know not," was my hesitating answer, and the tears could not be kept back—nor were they the tears of a boy. "He is waiting for you, he said."

"Ah! Then he will not have long to wait, methinks," Radisson breathed, holding the hand of Ruth. At sight of Grim I bethought me that he might well prove of service, and so I called him to follow me out to the front of the cave.

"Ready!" thrilled a sharp whisper from Swift Arrow, who had the guns close to his hand. Grim growled. This time the attack came with no forewarning until we saw the approach of the Chippewas, creeping stealthily forward through the snow. But as they came, arrows pattered around us from those behind, who covered their advance.

And this time, there was no stopping them. Five times did the Arrow fire, but then came a rush, and he had but time to draw his knife and put his tomahawk ready. I caught up one of the heavy fusils and swung it about my head, and then they were upon us—a mad swirl of men who seemed to spring out of the darkness and up the path to our ledge.

Now, when it came to hand-to-hand fighting, my great strength proved its worth. The Arrow had crawled to my side, and as only one or two men could reach us at a time, we managed to fling them back with gun-butt and tomahawk, while the shrill yell of the Mohawk rose madly over the shrieks of the Chippewas.

Time after time my heavy piece rose and fell, sometimes parried and sometimes not, while at my side glittered the steel of the old chief, rapid and deadly; but ever the voice of Gib urged on the warriors, and ever they pressed up that narrow path in mad resolve. On a sudden I felt a sharp pain in my shoulder, and the fusil dashed out of my hands against the rock wall as I staggered back.

An instant, and I had pulled out the knife with a shudder of pain, but that instant had been well-nigh fatal, for the Chippewas poured over us. Then, while I was still faint with the shock and the pain came Grim to the fore. Swift Arrow had risen to his feet, still plying his deadly steel desperately, when the great sheep-clog crouched and sprang, snarling and tearing in the midst of them beneath us.

The Chippewas fell back before him in wild affright, leaving two of their number at handgrips with us. One of these went down under the knife of the Mohawk; the other I seized by the throat and dashed back against the rock, where he lay silent. Then I whistled sharp and shrill, and Grim came back to me— bleeding and torn, but still not hurt unto death. So near had they come to taking us, that but for him we had assuredly perished.

But the Chippewas had not retreated far, and the evil tones of Gib showed me where he stood out there on the snow. The Arrow had fallen forward against the rock, helpless; when next they charged, his aid would be of no avail. And the blood was running fast from my shoulder, as I reloaded one of the weapons.

Gib was standing out in the center of the pass, and of a sudden I heard what seemed to be a bellow of rage, followed by a wild shriek from the Chippewas. Turning, I saw a mighty form leaping through the darkness—great horns outspread, giant shoulders rising high over the group of warriors, huge hoofs striking to right and left. In the dim light, I thought I saw Gib raise a musket, and for an instant the flash of it showed me the Mighty One himself, poised high in air as he leaped upon the terror-struck men. Then all went dark again. One horrible, long-drawn shriek wailed out down the great cliffs as I raised my musket and aimed at the huge shape below, from which men fled every way. I fired, and saw it stumble forward over a smaller form in the snow; then I felt the faintness of my wound come upon me again, and had but strength enough to stagger back through the cave, meet the staring eyes of Radisson, and fall at the feet of Ruth. But as I fell, I heard from without the war-cry of Uchichak, and knew that the Mighty One had saved us; then I fell asleep, with the tongue of Grim hot on my cheek.

CHAPTER XX

HOW PIERRE RADISSON SLEPT

W HEN I woke, it was in the midst of a grave silence. That may scarce mean sense, yet to the full it express-es the feeling that came upon me when I opened my eyes and looked about me. I was sitting against the cave wall, Ruth at my side, and Grim, his great honest dog's eyes full of pain, crouching and looking up at me.

Now the little cave was full of light and men—Uchichak and other chiefs of the Crees, who were standing silent before me, while the light smoke from the dry wood drove past us in the draught. Ruth was bathing my face with water, but I pushed her hand away. This silence among so many boded ill, and op-pressed me strangely. I remembered Radisson, and sought for him through the crowding forms.

He was sitting against the wall, with the Swift Arrow at his side, their hands clasped. But, although the Mohawk was well-nigh gone, never had Radisson's face seemed happier, younger and nobler. Hope leaped into my heart that he had not been as sore stricken as we had thought.

Ruth helped me to my feet. We went over and sat beside him. His hand closed on ours, and he smiled kindly on Ruth.

"Well does the Great Swift Arrow deserve his name," he said softly, so that the dying eyes of the old chief lit up. "He brought Uchichak to us and sped on ahead of him, and so saved us all."

"Then you are not so badly hurt?" I exclaimed joyfully. Radis-son chuckled, and made answer in his old rich, laughing voice.

"Hurt? Why, lad, I have triumphed! The Keeper, the Swift Arrow and I will travel the last trail together ere long, but see!" And he waved the paper of Hudson aloft as might a boy, then his eyes went to the Cree chiefs, and he spoke in their own tongue.

"My brothers, White Eagle goes upon the spirit-trail. But first he would tell you that in the days to come, white men shall arrive among you. Do not make war upon them, my brothers. They will trade with you for your furs, and will bring much good to you. Will you remember this?"

"We will remember," answered The Crane gravely, and a murmur passed around among the other chiefs. The head of Swift Arrow suddenly sank forward and his hand dropped from that of Radisson. The Mohawk had not waited.

Radisson's face never changed as he asked the Crees how the fight had gone, and if Gib had been slain, and then drew Ruth and me down to him while he waited the answer.

"My father," said Uchichak slowly, "the Crees did not fight, for the enemy had gone. The Mighty One had fought for us and scattered them. But—" and he hesitated an instant, "as we came near, a gun was fired from the cave, and lightning shot across the snow. When we had sought the Chippewas, we found the Mighty One lying dead, and beneath his hoofs was the form of The Pike."

Uchichak paused. With a little shudder I remembered how I had seen the giant moose uprearing and striking out with hoofs and horns, and how he had stumbled across a man even as I fired. Ruth was sobbing quietly on Radisson's shoulder, and the old wanderer addressed us in English.

"Children, do not grieve. I am an old man, and have lived through more than most men. As for Gib, he has perished by the hand of God, even as I foretold that he would. Now listen carefully.

"You, Ruth, are of right named Marie de Courbelles. It were best to visit Montreal and Quebec, for there live your father's people, though he is dead long since, and there you may obtain your inheritance, which is a goodly one."

Ruth sobbed out that she wanted none of it, whereat the old man petted her head and smiled on me suddenly.

"Davie, you will care for the little maid?"

"An' she will let me, I will," was my low reply.

"Then I shall pass happy," and Radisson sighed as if a burden was off his mind. "I would that you had the old Bible of which you spoke, lass. I would like to hear once more the story of those days Christ spent in the wilderness. It hath ever attracted me strangely—I would that my days had been set where I might have known Him!"

And as Radisson voiced the age-old wish of the world, I bethought me that I still had the packet which The Keeper had put in my hands, and so drew it out hastily.

"I have it here—read it, Ruth!"

The little maid took the Book with trembling hands. The translation was Englished by Wicliff, and when she had found the place she put it into French again for Radisson. He listened gravely, his head drooping while she read, the stately chiefs standing around in silent attention, though they understood it not. When it was finished he sighed again.

"Thanks, my daughter. Brave Eyes, help me to my feet, for I would fain look upon the face of Hudson ere I pass."

With The Crane, I helped him to gain his feet, and he leaned heavily upon us. I motioned Ruth not to follow, for that sight was none for her eyes, and so we led him through the inner passage to the second chamber where sat the great mariner in his eternal silence. The glow from our torch lit up his face, and Radisson sank down against the table.

"Henry Hudson and Pierre Radisson!" I heard him murmur. "It were a fitting ending, and a noble one!" Pulling himself up, he signed to us that we should help him back again, which we did, nothing loath. Uchichak was trembling when we reached the outer cave, for that man who sat with quill in hand had frighted him mightily. Yet Radisson had been more observing than I, for all his weakness.

"Davie," he said, more faintly, when he was again sitting upon the skins, "I wish that you do one more thing for me. When I have entered upon the spirit-trail, then carry me into that chamber and let me sit at the table over against Henry Hudson. Place there The Keeper and The Swift Arrow also, for such greatness is worthy them.

"That keg upon the table holds powder, I think. When we are placed, lad, do you set that keg of powder in the narrow entrance and—"

He went no farther, for Ruth fell upon his neck with a great cry. But he knew that I had understood, and that I would obey. Nothing could better show the fantastic, grim spirit of the old wanderer than this last desire of his—to be tombed in the living rock, with Henry Hudson and the two Mohawks beside him. Nor, as I think now, was it so mad a wish after all; for what better tomb could Pierre Radisson have, in all this land he had found and loved and given to the world?

Now, since we had to pass the night here at least, I had the body of Swift Arrow carried within the second chamber. The Crees had already formed a camp outside, and as Radisson wished to taste fresh meat once more before he passed—for we had gone hungry of late, through having brought little food with us—I went outside with Uchichak. The Cree camp was in a place sheltered from the terrific, howling wind, and as the fires in the sky had now risen high overhead and sent down a ghostly light into the deep gulch, I was enabled to see the Mighty One where he lay—for the Indians had not dared to touch him.

That last chance shot of mine had pierced through his heart, striking him just behind the shoulder and going true. And what a great beast he was! I had shot moose ere this, with my arrows, and had seen full many, but never so huge a beast as this Mighty One. Still beneath his great body lay Gib o' Clarclach, his evil face untouched and grinning its last defiant grin up at the sky which he had blasphemed.

In that moment I was glad that no blow of mine had laid him low. He had lived wrongly, and died wrongly. What a contrast between his death and that of The Keeper! Yet the white man was of a race which we call superior, he knew of things which the Mohawk had never dreamed of, he had had advantages which The Keeper could never have had—and he had lost his soul alive. Nay, I am not judging him, God forbid! It, may be that even such as he are not without hope elsewhere.

Uchichak plucked up his courage and together we cut off the choicest portions of the giant moose and carried them over to the fires of the camp in the shelter of the walls. Many of the Crees had gone on to the lodges, there to rescue Laughing Snow and to await the coming of Talking Owl from the western pass.

When the meat was cooked I carried it back to the cavern, where we found Radisson as we had left him, and but for his weakness I had never known that he was hurt. He seemed to have become twenty years younger in an hour.

Only Uchichak and one of two of the older chiefs had remained with us. We all partook of the meat, and I even forced a portion upon Ruth, who was in sore need of it. She, poor girl, had little heart for eating, but managed to do well enough, as did we all.

"Now let us consider," said Radisson, to whom the meal had given strength. Not even when he was facing death would he give up planning. "How are you to reach home again?"

"We have no home," said Ruth sadly.

"Ayrby is sold, and we may not return."

"Tut, child," he responded. "I make no doubt you can get the farm back again, if so you wish. Once I am gone, neither English nor French will molest you. Indeed, you might make for the nearest post and there take ship for the colonies. I would have you visit Montreal, if possible, and there regain the inheritance which awaits you. There will be ships in the Bay from Boston, mayhap, who will set forth in the spring."

Straight upon this there entered four warriors who bore the silent form of The Keeper. Radisson demanded to look upon the face of his friend once more, and I would have drawn Ruth aside, but she would not. And when The Keeper's face was uncovered, I was glad that this was so; for the noble old face was strangely exalted and lit with a great beauty such as never in all my life had I seen. I cannot describe it fittingly, yet it was a memory that has ever remained fresh and vivid—as if God's hand had touched the worn features lightly, ere they fell into the repose of death.

Then they covered him again and bore him into the inner chamber, where they stayed no longer than might be. The old wanderer, I could see, was now sinking fast, and his hand would tremble as it clutched mine and Ruth's. Presently he pulled from about his neck a gold medal—the same, it proved, that had been given him long years before by the English king, ere his shameful betrayal. This he pressed into Ruth's hand.

"Here, my daughter—keep this in my memory, and with my blessing. It is a poor thing to remember me by, and yet it is all I have; it is the sole trace of honor that has come to me for all my labors, and I would that you keep it always."

"Oh, we need naught to remember—" began Ruth, but ended in a sob. Perhaps to check her grief, Radisson asked her to read to him from the Book, and so she took it up again and after a little began to read, while the tears ran over her cheeks. Whether by accident or by design she never told me, but the passage was that wherein the prophet met and spoke with his God upon the mountain.

I watched Radisson as she read, and saw his face light up, then the look passed into one of awe and wonder. Slowly his head bowed down, until I checked Ruth with my hand, for I thought that the end had come; but it was not so, for he signed to her to continue, and raised his head once more, looking up at the roof of the cave with startled eyes, as though he saw there more than the bare rock. And with that he stretched out his arm, and I helped him to his feet. He shook me off and took one step forward alone.

"Not in the whirlwind," he cried passionately, his voice ringing deep echoes from all around, "not in the whirlwind, O Lord, nor in the fire, nor in the storm have I found Thee! But in the—still—small—"

He swayed forward, all the life gone out of him suddenly, and when I lowered him to the skins I knew that Radisson had departed upon the spirit-trail. I signed to The Crane, and we carried him into the inner chamber and seated him across the table from Hudson. Then—for I knew that in the morning no power would tempt me to enter that room again—I carried out the keg, which proved to be nearly full of coarse, dry powder, and left it in the passage.

"Come," said Ruth, catching at my arm, "we will sleep out by the fire. Here I—I cannot, Davie."

I held her to me for a moment, then told The Crane to lead her to the fire. When she had gone I gathered up the skins and furs, and after a little time we had fixed up a shelter for her in a cranny of the rocks, where I left her. I rejoined the silent Crees and flung myself down in the warmth of the fire to sleep, for I was very weary.

The day was high when I wakened. Ruth, it seemed, was still asleep. In the early morning the band of Talking Owl had arrived, and with Uchichak's warriors had swept away those that remained of the Chippewas. The days of the band were over; few ever returned to their villages, and those that did bore with them such a tale as kept Chippewa hunters in their own country for many winters to come.

My first duty before Ruth was up, was to clear away all signs of conflict. Gib and his dead were laid to rest in the outer cave, decently enough. The giant moose had already been quartered and the great antlers were preserved for me as trophies. So when

Ruth appeared, naught remained of the struggle save the trampled snow and a few shattered fragments of arrows.

The Crees were anxious to be home again, having raided the lodges in the basin and burned them. So without delay I whistled Grim and entered the cave. Placing the keg of powder in the narrowest part of the entrance, I set a long train with a final fuse of birch bark. When all was ready I warned off the curious Crees and lit the bark with a stick from the fire.

For a moment it blazed up, and when I had turned from my hasty flight I saw only a tiny flicker of flame from the powder. Then came a cloud of smoke from the entrance, a low, thunderous roar that reverberated from the high cliffs overhead, and the great rocks crashed down in utter ruin. The cave was no more. Pierre Radisson slept with those whom he had chosen for company in his last long sleep.

CHAPTER XXI

THE SHADOW OF THE CROSS

WITH SADDENED hearts we turned our faces toward the Barren Places once again. Swift Arrow had killed two of the dogs in his dash for help, but the others were sufficient to draw the sled bearing Grim and Ruth. The old dog's wounds had become too stiff and sore to permit of his traveling afoot, so he curled up at Ruth's feet.

The antlers of the Mighty One were lashed to the sled behind the little maid, forming a rest for her to lean back upon. My wound did not prevent traveling, and there was no great need of haste. A band of the warriors pushed on to provide food for us who followed, and at length we emerged from that dismal, howling passage through the cliffs into the frozen silence of the desolate wastes.

Not until the second evening did we reach the village once more. On the journey I initiated Uchichak into the mysteries of a musket, for although the Crees had often seen our guns and knew their uses, they had never heard them fired until that shot wherewith I killed the Mighty One. The chief was delighted with the weapon which I gave to him, as were the other chiefs, for I kept only one fusil for my own use.

At the village the party of Talking Owl remained for a great feast. On the second evening of this feast a great council was held of the two bands, for so Ruth had urged upon me that day.

"We must not forget. Davie, that our task is not finished here," she said gravely, as we were discussing what we had best do. "See if you can get them to admit me to a Council again, to read to them from the Book. I can put it into Cree, I think."

So we crowded into the lodge of council in the evening, and among others who were admitted was Soan-ge-ta-ha the Chippewa. The destruction of his band and the death of Gib seemed to have broken the old chief, and he had readily agreed to return home in peace and to lead no more war-parties into the Ghost Hills. Three of the foremost seats, however, were left empty out of respect, while from the top of the lodge was suspended the great pair of antlers which the giant moose had borne. The first who addressed the Council was Uchichak, when the calumet had been ceremoniously passed around, Brave Heart accepting it in silence.

"My brothers," he began gravely, "once before has Yellow Lily been admitted to the Council. Then she told us about the Great Spirit and His Son, and about the Book, of which we understood little. But in the Ghost Hills, my brothers, she found this same paper-talk, sent to her by the Great Spirit, and she wishes that we should hear it.

"My brothers, I am old. I have seen the Mighty One fall under the hand of Brave Eyes. I do not know whether our Great Spirit sent him or not, but we decreed in Council that if he slew the Mighty One, then would we listen to his Great Spirit."

Uchichak resumed his seat. Talking Owl and his chiefs, who had of course heard the tale of the previous Council, objected to allowing Ruth or any other woman to enter the lodge. They were, however, overruled, and finally assented.

When Ruth entered, she stood beside the fire so that the flickering light would enable her to read from the little Book. I had not known what portion she would give to them, but she started with the Creation, wisely enough. Then she selected parts of the Gospels which gave short sketches from the life of the Master, and concluded with the great story of Saint Paul. She turned the whole into Cree as she went, stumbling in places where she knew no words, altering other parts to simpler language, but on the whole the chiefs understood and listened absorbedly. They were little more than children in spirit, loving a story for its own sake, but over-quick to catch the sense of a parable, so that Ruth read them many of these.

It was a lengthy reading, and when it was done I had thought the chiefs were asleep but for their glittering eyes centered on the little maid. When I had led her out and come back to my seat there was a very long silence, until at last the oldest chief stepped out and made the smoke-offering to the four corners of the heavens.

"My brothers, there were four chiefs who sat in the Council, and who defied the Mighty One, saying that he was not sent by the Great Spirit to us his children. My eyes are very feeble, yet I see only one of these four. There are three vacant places before me. Perhaps White Eagle and the Brothers of the Thunder have not yet come?"

His gaze swept around as if looking for the absent ones, but none answered.

"My brothers, I see before me Brave Eyes, whose name shall be Moose-slayer hereafter. Over his head swing the horns of the Mighty One. I am too old to take the war-trail, and my limbs are feeble. Perhaps Moose-slayer will tell me how the Mighty One was slain."

A whisper of approval passed around as he sat clown, and after a little the eyes of the chiefs were fixed upon me, waiting. So, when the silence had become unendurable, I came to my feet and faced them.

Painting the picture before them as well as I might, for so they love to have their stories told. I related how The Keeper had died beneath the Chippewa arrows, a martyr to his faith, and retold his words. Then on to the fight at the cavern and the silent man whom we had found sitting therein, and I laid emphasis on how the little Bible had been his, telling them something of his life. I concluded the whole by reciting the death of the Mighty One, which had brought me the high honor of a new name. I urged naught upon them, merely pointing out how the Great Spirit had directed my bullet to its mark, and so made an end of speaking. I could tell that my words had impressed them, but I did not know how deeply until Uchichak arose.

"My brothers, we have listened to the Yellow Lily, we have heard the words of Moose-slayer," for such is the best translation I can give of the Cree term applied to me. "I have never met the dead, my brothers, yet in the paper-talk the Great Spirit has said that we should meet them upon the spirit-trail. I would like to meet White Eagle once again, and my father Gray Fish, and my other friends and kinsmen. Our hearts are open; but first I would listen to the words of Talking Owl."

The latter chief, who was gaunt and hollow-eyed, surprised me greatly by his words.

"There can be but one Great Spirit, my brothers. The Crane has told you that our hearts are open, and it is true. The Mighty One was very strong. Our young men dared not stand against him, and our old men said that he was a messenger from the Great Spirit. We believed that this was true.

"Then came this white man to our villages. We hunted with him, and we found that his tongue was straight. When he told The Crane that the Mighty One was not sent by the Great Spirit and that he would hunt the moose, we were sorry, for we loved him and we loved White Eagle his brother. The Chippewas, my brothers, believed in our Great Spirit, yet the Mighty One attacked and scattered them, and the white man slew him in a moment. Talking Owl thinks that the Great Spirit of the white man and the Great Spirit of the red man are the same, and that He has sent Moose-slayer as a messenger to us."

With that I knew that the cause was won. The Council lasted a great while longer, each of the older chiefs speaking in turn while the warriors listened, but they all agreed with Uchichak and Talking Owl, and in the end it was decided that they should accept the "sign in the water" at another council to be held the next night.

She selected parts of the Gospels— The chiefs
understood and listened absobedly.

I hastened back to Ruth with the good news, and she was
mightily rejoiced. As it was late, we made no preparations until
the next day. The Crees had decided that Soan-ge-ta-ha should
return scatheless to his people, but somewhat to my surprise
the Chippewa announced that he, too, would receive the "sign
in the water" with the Cree chiefs. This was more than we had

looked for, and it greatly strengthened our influence, for Brave Heart was a famous chief in his own nation.

So in the great council-lodge we met and there the chiefs and warriors received baptism. I felt keenly mine own unworthiness in the matter, but for this there was no help. The squaws could by no means enter this lodge, and so we visited them outside by the light of great fires, afterward returning to the Council. There I set before them all, the fact that it was time that Ruth and I returned to our own people.

"The spirit of White Eagle will be very happy," I told them, "as he looks down and sees that you also are followers of the Great Spirit, my brothers. And now that we have fulfilled our mission, we would fain depart. First, however, I bid you to send messengers to all the other villages, and cement a League of Peace here in the northland, a silver chain of peace which shall bind you together strongly. You shall have a council from all your tribes and villages which shall rule you justly, and if this be done there shall no war or danger come upon you for ever. I would fain stay and see that this is done rightly, yet I am far from mine own people and my home, and the trail is a long one to follow."

As you may imagine, Uchichak and the rest were in huge consternation at this, but in the end they promised to follow my advice and form a peace-league among the peoples of the snows. Whether this was ever done I know not to this day.

As to the manner of our return, few of the Crees hereabouts had ever visited the shores of the Great Bay, for the trail led across the Barren Places and their hunting grounds lay rather to the west and south. Soan-ge-ta-ha, however, offered to guide us to one of the posts as soon as we should come to the Chippewa country, and this offer we accepted right willingly.

Talking Owl and his warriors remained a few days longer for a last grand hunt, and a dozen Crees, with Uchichak, arranged to accompany us to the Chippewa country. When the time of parting came, I told them that if possible I would send other messengers to them from the Great Spirit, who should tell them more of Him than could I; but I laid no great weight upon this promise, knowing the men who made up the Adventurers, and indeed the first to come among them with the Word after our leaving, were missionaries from the Canadas.

So once more we turned our backs upon friends and faced, this time eastward, the waste places. The trip to the Chippewa country was a hard one, but Ruth got through it well enough and Grim remained constant at our side. At the Chippewa villages we parted with Uchichak, and there still hang upon the wall before me the magnificent moccasins which he gave me as a parting gift, while to Ruth was given a shirt of doeskin with quill workings in many hues.

Brave Heart kept his promises faithfully, although the Chippewas were bitter against us for the loss of so large a party, and with some of his men led us eastward, thinking to hit upon the Bay and so cross the ice to Albany. But to the post we never came, for we had no sooner come to the Bay, a desolate waste of ice stretching into the distance, than we saw a smoke from a river-mouth, and when we had come to it found there a ship laid up for the winter, and near the ship a little fortified camp of men.

I left our party and advanced down the slope toward them, and when our coming was seen, a man came forth to meet me, while over the camp was run up the flag of France. The man was also French, and I greeted him in his own tongue, asking for refuge and shelter. He tendered us a warm greeting, and therewith we went down to the camp, wondering how this ship of France came to be in the territory of the Adventurers.

CHAPTER XXII

THE END OF THE LONG TRAIL

IT WAS simple enough. The ship was the barque Pelican, out of New France, and her company were fur-pirates in the Bay. They had been caught by the ice, but as none at the Company's posts knew of their presence, they were safe enough. In the barque was great store of furs bartered from the Indians, and her master, one de Croissac, sought only to win home again safe ere the Company's ships came from England in the spring.

They were warm-hearted men, these Frenchmen, and gave us of their best. I told de Croissac all our tale, whereat he marveled much, and promised to take us safe to Montreal, whence we could get ship for France or New England, and so home again. Moreover, he knew of the de Courbelles, and that Ruth's heritance was great.

This troubled me no little. At last the spring came and the ice went out in its warmth, and the "Pelican" was ready. On the day we sailed. Ruth and I stood on the hilltop above, gazing out across the land and the water.

"Somewhere in that ice-dotted blue," Ruth said softly, "sleeps the 'Lass o' Dee,' with all those whom we knew and loved, Davie."

"Yes," I made heavy-hearted answer, "and we leave them here for ever. When we get to New France, and you become a great lady, Ruth, I will leave you there also among your kin, and go—where I know not."

"Why, Davie," and she slipped her hand into mine gently, "do you think so hard of me as to leave me among strangers? I had thought we would go back to Ayrby together—"

"Lass, lass," I cried out in the old Gaelic we had not spoke for so long, "an' you stay in New France you shall be a great lady, rich and be-suitored. Would you then come back to the little stead on the moors, where wealth is naught, where all is rude and homely and—"

"Yes, Davie," she whispered, "because it is rude and homely and—beautiful, I love it. So you thought I had rather be a great lady! Truly, you might have known me better than that."

Aye, and I had, but I had wished for her to say it. So we stood for long, until a gun crashed out from the "Pelican," warning us to come. As we turned to go, I caught her to me and my heart swelled with the knowledge that though the New World had taken much from me, it had in the end given me more a thousandfold.

In the Straits we were sighted by an English ship, but the "Pelican" was too fast for her, and not another sail did we see until we reached New France and were safe. De Croissac, who knew our story and our love, advised that we be married before seeking out Ruth's people, for were our story and the ending of Radisson to become known, there was no telling but that she might be sent to France as a ward of the Governor.

So it came about that we stepped ashore and sought out a friend of the kindly captain, a priest whose little chapel nestled in the shadow of the citadel, and from which we went as man and wife, soberly and happily.

Before leaving the Bay, Soan-ge-ta-ha had conveyed to me a parting gift from Uchichak and the Crees, in the shape of a packet of furs. These I had not opened until the cargo of the "Pelican" came to be examined, when it was found that they were of the choicest beaver and fox, and that their sale would afford us much ready money.

Thus it chanced that when we left Montreal for Boston town, aboard a trader of that port, both Ruth and I were like to be well off upon our return to the Old World. Of the finding of Hudson I had said nothing, keeping the little Bible and the scrap of written paper safe stowed away, for our tale seemed wild enough as it was, in all sooth.

One more package there was, in two pieces, but very large and bulky. What this contained I did not know. It had been Ruth's secret from the time we left Uchichak's village until we reached Rathesby once again, and so on to the stead at Ayrby, which Ian MacDonald yielded up readily enough, being glad to go back to his nets. At the unpacking of this thing, Ruth bade me begone for a time. I returned from the moors to find, hung over the broad fireplace, the massy antlers of the Mighty One! She had fetched them where I had clean forgot them, to be a lasting memorial of the days that had been.

So here endeth my tale. There is another Grim now to tend the sheep, yet still about us are things whereby to remember him and his. But the things we fetched back from the New World were more than we had gone to seek there. We had dreamed of fortune, and we came home with love. We had looked for struggle and hardship, and we had found them, but we had come home again with peace. Ruth, bending over my shoulder as I write this last, would have me say one word more of Radisson—nay, she shall write it herself, here at the end.

"Trust thou in the Lord, wait patiently for Him, and He shall give thee thy heart's desire!"

ABOUT THE AUTHOR

H. BEDFORD-JONES is a Canadian by birth, but not by profession, having removed to the United States at the age of one year. For over twenty years he has been more or less profitably engaged in writing and traveling. As he has seldom resided in one place longer than a year or so and is a person of retiring habits, he is somewhat a man of mystery; more than once he has suffered from unscrupulous gentlemen who impersonated him—one of whom murdered a wife and was subsequently shot by the police, luckily after losing his alias.

The real Bedford-Jones is an elderly man, whose gray hair and precise attire give him rather the appearance of a retired foreign diplomat. His hobby is stamp collecting, and his collection of Japan is said to be one of the finest in existence. At present writing he is en route to Morocco, and when this appears in print he will probably be somewhere on the Mojave Desert in company with Erle Stanley Gardner.

Questioned as to the main facts in his life, he declared there was only one main fact, but it was not for publication; that his life had been uneventful except for numerous financial losses, and that his only adventures lay in evading adventurers. In his younger years he was something of an athlete, but the encroachments of age preclude any active pursuits except that of motoring. He is usually to be found poring over his stamps, working at his typewriter, or laboring in his California rose garden, which is one of the sights of Cathedral Cañon, near Palm Springs.